Russell Celyn Jones is the author of *Small Times*, *An Interference of Light* and *The Eros Hunter*. He has taught at the universities of Iowa, USA; East Anglia; and the Western Cape, South Africa. He lives in London and is a regular book reviewer for *The Times*.

Also by Russell Celyn Jones

Small Times
An Interference of Light
The Eros Hunter

SOLDIERS AND INNOCENTS

Russell Celyn Jones

An *Abacus* Book

First published in Great Britain by Jonathan Cape Ltd 1990
First published by Abacus 1998

A CIP catalogue record for this book
is available from the British Library.

ISBN 0 349 11043 3

Typeset in Cheltenham Book by
Palimpsest Book Production Limited,
Polmont, Stirlingshire
Printed and bound in Great Britain by
Clays Ltd, St Ives plc.

Abacus
A Division of
Little, Brown and Company (UK)
Brettenham House
Lancaster Place
London WC2E 7EN

For Rebecca Grace Jones

I would like to thank Caroline Dawnay and Tom Maschler; my parents, Grace and Richard Jones, and my sisters, Diane and Angela; Katherine, Daniel and Robert Coyle, Brian Thomas, Jonathon Lewis, Trajan and Darius Hague, Ruth, Carol, Dafydd, Helen, Dilys, Eunice and Dewi Griffiths, Cheryl Pearl Sucher, Joanna and Peter Llewelyn, Jane and Anthony Browne, Sally Minogue, Peter Epps, Jamie Lehrer. Finally I am most in debt to Peter Austin Lewis, formerly of Two Para.

They just couldn't see even six inches in front of their faces on account of the ringing downpour and a ground mist thickening around their waists. Visibility had been so good, too, just an hour before, with the moon in its first quarter high-lighting the rims of the purple hills. Now the dark had solidified, resisting all efforts to be pushed aside by the men closing in on the derelict farmhouse, navigating less by sight than by hindsight.

Fifty metres short of the farmhouse a white owl flew from a tree, clearing their heads by an arm's length. The Captain had never seen a white owl before and it distracted him from his mission. He watched it vanishing through the ceiling of low cloud, a big bird labouring to gain altitude, and his eyes filled with soft rain. For that moment the weight of his waterlogged smock and webbing equipment lifted right off his body, and left him feeling unbalanced.

It was all so potent. Something scuttled away from them in the field. A goat, or possibly a sheep. But it counted, whatever it was. There were two lessons this conflict had taught him: All the army ever did was chase shadows. None of those shadows was innocent.

A torchlight flashed briefly in a window at the farmhouse. Someone behind him discharged a round from his rifle. Whether by accident or frustration, it cued the machine gun section holding a flank position even further behind to put down fire through the same window. One of their rounds was a tracer and suddenly the Captain could see who he was running with: a cadre of spectral teenagers through a field of sheep.

The farmhouse was a gutted charcoaled pit strewn with timbers and the flotsam of an itinerant people. There were no doors – the soldiers came through holes in the wall, no window glass, no roof. Standing ceremoniously in the centre of things was a pinball machine, smashed and dented, except . . . miraculously perhaps . . . for the tropical island scene painted on its glass panel; coconut trees, monkeys, women in grass skirts, and the sea. A single strip of corrugated tin flapped in the roof beams and threatened to come crashing down. Mingling together in the air were smells of woodsmoke and cordite. A tracer round embedded and fizzling in the brickwork shone light on a tarpaulin sheet, stretched over a taut rope and forming a bender tent. The Captain lifted the flap with the muzzle of his rifle. He could make out a stove under the sheet, fashioned from an oil drum and propped up on bricks. It belched out thick acrid smoke and he had to squeeze out the tears to see further inside, to a body lying on a mattress of foam rubber. It was a naked woman who had been shot in the head by one of their rounds.

There was someone else in there with the body. The Captain backed out sharply as the riflemen zeroed in on the entrance to the tent. He slung his rifle behind his head and produced a side arm, pulling back the slide to send a bullet into the chamber. He felt safer with a handgun, preferred the manoeuvrability of a Browning 9mm at close quarters.

A woman carefully emerged from underneath the tarpaulin. She was wearing a black skirt torn to ribbons and a school blazer, bordered with orange cord, sporting a badge on the breast pocket – of the world globe. The woman was middle-aged, corpulent, her long bushy hair caught in mid-flight by a ribbon. She took a few steps towards the Captain, the rain flinging mud around her ankles, and extended her arms to him. He backed away, straining to see what the object was in her outstretched hands. And then he realised with a sharp jolt that the woman was offering him a baby, a stillborn infant coated in blood and mucus. Their arrival had coincided with the birth of a dead child.

ONE

The sky had been gouged into a dome of gun-metal greyness by morning. Stooped figures left the town and returned to their moorings to inspect the storm damage. The sea beyond the harbour was white going on blue. On the headland in the marshes a resurrection of nature was occurring as birds appeared in the sky again and wild flowers stiffened their spines.

Evan Price pushed his son on a bicycle across the marshes, the boy's ecstatic cries underlining the melody of the birds. His feet were six inches short of the pedals and he bounced in the saddle. His laughter seemed to intoxicate his father, who accelerated past the broken saplings, his feet skidding in the moist earth. 'Now go round the tree!'

'Right you are, Terence.'

'Not there. I said up there!'

Evan broke into a fierce gallop on a long run. Terence tensed and became silent, the pedals spinning into a blur. A Harrier squadron gaining altitude out of Pembrey rent the sky, filling all the air with their music.

Evan gave the bike a thrust before releasing his hold on the saddle. In cartoon sequence, with legs stuck out to the sides, Terence freewheeled the machine he had not yet discovered how to stop into the bough of a sapling. Evan ran over to where the bike had come to an abrupt end to its run and untangled his son from the steel. He raised Terence and the boy cried in his arms. 'I'm not your friend any more!'

'I'm sorry, I lost my grip.' And Evan was sorry, even if he hadn't lost his grip. He was enjoying this, by Christ, the unlimited, unpoliced freedom.

The boy sobbed into the nape of his father's neck, moistening the hairs of his beard with saliva. A refrain from some elder's wisdom entered Evan's head: Conquer a child's fear while it is still burning. Evan remounted his son and pushed him even faster than before. 'Don't go so fast. I said don't go so fast! . . . I want to get off . . .'

Evan had settled into an easy stride. He could run like that all day. After all, his body was fashioned for rigorous movement, trained for flight, and his muscles twitched with pleasure. Words of a psalm popped onto his tongue. 'Yea, though I walk through the valley of the shadow of death, I shall fear no evil,' he sang. 'Psalm 43, old man,' Evan misinformed Terence. He followed the psalm with a poem.

> 'The man who fears war and squats opposing
> My words for stour, hath no blood of crimson
> But is fit only to rot in womanish peace

... That's a man now in hell, Terence. There's some more ...

> Come let's to music! I have no life
> Save when the swords clash.
> And I love to see the sun rise blood-crimson.
> And I watch his spears through the dark clash
> And it fills my heart with rejoicing
> And pries wide my mouth with fast music
> When I see him so scorn and defy peace
> His lone might 'gainst all darkness opposing.'

It took a minute to register with him that Terence was far from happy with the action. His mouth was a quivering silent zero, his head tossed back like a dumped marionette severed from strings.

Evan plucked the boy from the saddle and let the bike travel and fall. Terence punched his father in the ear. 'I said I wanted to get off! I'm not your friend any more.'

'I'm sorry, Terence. Your old man is out of practice.'

*   *   *

7

The road through the marshes had no pavement and Evan walked on tarmac beside Terence mounted on his bike. He was a small five-year-old who could have fitted inside Evan's jacket. A well dressed child in turquoise corduroys, red shoes and a custom-knitted sweater emblazoned with animals. His duffel coat was falling off his narrow shoulders. At a glance you could tell his father hadn't tailored him, dressed as he was in cheap denims, a shirt with no collar and wide-lapelled suit jacket. He inhaled the scent of coconut shampoo from Terence's head and noticed how all his hair sprang from a point at the back of his head, a source of great energy.

Terence, as if making up for time lost, began to ask his father all manner of questions.

'What's a prince?'

'A figurehead of the Armed Forces.'

'What's he do?'

'Nothing really.'

'Just buys lots and lots of things?'

'Yeah – jewellery, castles . . .'

'And he's got a big box of money?'

'Yes, Terence.'

'Full up to the top?'

Evan swept Terence and the bike off the road as an oncoming car, a police car, a white Ford Sierra, approached at speed. Evan rigorously avoided eye-contact with the policemen as the car decelerated.

The driver's hand came out of the side window to wave at them before passing. 'Why did he wave, daddy?'

'It's called courtesy, Terence. Mark it well.'

Long after the car had gone, the policeman's unsmiling face lingered behind. Evan grew cold all over. The bulk of steel in his pocket felt hot against the flesh of his thigh.

'Can you go on living after you die?' Terence continued with the conversation as they continued with the ride.

'I don't know. But I feel I should warn you: you'd be different. Like a dog or a ghost.'

'A ghost?'

'Yes, a ghost, old man.'

'I've seen a ghost.'

'So have I. There's plenty of them about . . . sorry, didn't mean to steal your thunder. What colour was the ghost you saw?'

'Green.'

'Really? Mine too.'

'When do you die?'

'Depends on what you do for a living. Depends on what people around you do for a living.'

'When will you die?'

'Any day now. Could be tomorrow.'

'Will I die tomorrow?'

'No. No . . .' But Evan could not sound convincing.

The deserted road began to feel dangerous and Evan felt the shame of a parent who couldn't guarantee his child's safety.

Evan steered the bike across grass towards a wood nestling on the marshes. They entered the wood past a gamekeeper's cottage, where dead foxes hung from nails on the door. Evan passed silently, trying not to rustle the grass. Two black labradors emerged from undergrowth. They charged through an astonishingly green stagnant pond – straight at Evan and Terence. They wolfed down air, saliva elasticised upon their open jaws. Evan picked Terence out of the saddle and held him aloft, above his own head. The dogs passed each side, defusing counterfeit fury, and sniffed the turf around Evan's feet.

The gamekeeper crossed from his cottage to a red Toyota pick-up parked in the courtyard. A pump-action shotgun hung in the back window. The dogs returned to his side, shaking water off their coats as he unloaded sacks from the back of his pick-up. Evan noticed that he only had one arm, the sleeve of his thorn-proof jacket pinned to his side. He took a sack into the cottage, not once looking at the strangers. But he knew they were there; Evan saw that he was as tense as a cat.

As soon as his feet touched ground, Terence ran up to an enclosure of pheasants. He rattled the wire and the birds flew neurotically down the other end.

The gamekeeper returned. 'You're making the birds nervous. Can't you manage the kid?'

Evan walked Terence into the woods, pushing the bicycle. 'Why was he cross with us, daddy?'

'The man who kills his own flock always cares for the way they feel.'

In the woods Evan and Terence crushed bluebells underfoot. Evan was conscious of the beauty of a blue vein within a forest still fevered by winter, but equally conscious of the noise of their footfalls and Terence's raised voice. If was too much noise. Terence swept through the woods with a sycamore branch, scything the wild flowers.

Evan scanned the boughs with simple single sight. 'Look at the way the moss grows on the north side of the trees,' he tried to distract Terence. But Terence was not listening. He was caught up in a drama of destruction banging inside his little head.

'I'm going to fight the Germans,' he shouted. The poor Germans, Evan thought, were still taking flak after all these years, still every boy's imaginary enemy; not the Argentinians, not the Irish.

Terence ran ahead and began plucking clumps of bluebells.

'They'll die if you pick them,' Evan advised.

'I want to give them to Mummy.'

'I like flowers too, Terence.'

'They're for Mummy.'

11

'Mummy is out of the picture for a while.'

'Can't I see Mummy again?'

'Don't count on it, old man.'

Terence bolted away from Evan, putting a distance between them. It felt like a canyon. He leaned against a tree, lit a cigarette and drew deeply on the evolving scenario. It was a new experience having Terence around all the time, where he could see him, without supervision. It was similar to how he had felt in a car alone for the first time after passing his driving test. Exhilarating and frightening with so much solo power at your hands.

Evan watched his son picking more bluebells, walking deeper into the throat of the wood and finally out of sight. Evan stared at the cigarette in his fingers. It was time to give up smoking, he thought, before he wrecked his body, his physical gifts. His body had kept him alive, was his greatest ally.

He heard Terence call his name. 'Daddy . . . Daddy!'

How wonderful that sounded. It was a rank to be proud of. Terence's voice began to tremble before Evan could sober up sufficiently to answer. 'Here I am, Terence.'

Terence ran back into view like a happy puppy who had lost but now found his master again. Terence ran all the way to where his father stood smoking, and jumped up into his arms. Evan swung him around and around until his head grew dizzy and his eyes fogged over with tears.

TWO

The town of Creosor was a benign little dreamworld by the sea, populated by sleepwalkers. Each summer the place was clotted by holiday makers and their industry. Now, in the tail-end of winter, Creosor was a cadaver. The pastel coloured terraces of video and pinball palaces, discos, bingo arcades were shut down, mute. Salmon, turquoise, pink and ice-blue façades, as doubtful as a film set, sparkled in the cold sunlight. Coloured bulbs strung from lamp-posts looked anaemic. Evan Price pushed his son on his bike along the promenade. In the sand below, pigeons, gulls and sparrows squabbled and poked around in the huge piles of timber that had been hurled up against the sea wall – timbers of the Victorian pier wrecked during the storm. A lifeboat house, formerly attached to the pier, was isolated out at sea, its windows smashed, roof blown off. Structureless. Adrift. A group of skinheads had built a big bonfire with some of the timbers. The youths wore the same jungle-green bomber jackets, braces dangling like harness straps from their waists, heads shaven into smears. Their posturing was crude and obvious to Evan, who could feel the heat of the fire as they passed by along the promenade.

In the aftermath of a storm, Creosor was like a funeral town. The air was filled with acrid smoke and ash, the bad breath of a spent gale. It made Evan shiver as though he had entered a time-warp. Not his time at all.

'Creosor means Cursèd Hour, Terence. Let's see if I can remember the story. It's of Roman origin. The Welsh have a woman in their annals somewhere, called Helen, who used to ride out with a Roman general during the occupation. It was her who named this place. They were leading a column past here and had just got round a lake where a giant lived, a real giant. Helen's son was on a mount in the rear and as the last few soldiers were putting the lake behind them, the giant shot an arrow and killed her son. A soldier galloped down the ten-mile column and told Helen. She dismounted right where we are standing, fell on her knees and wept: Creosor! Creosor!'

'Were all these shops and lights here then?'

14

'She must have seen them coming, I think. Don't you, old man?'

A grey concrete block of flats stained by rain looked as if it were streaming with tears. Motley curtains were draped in every window. With their backs to the flats they approached the marina, where a cluster of masts filled the skyline. Rigging, agitated by wind, tapped out the same relentless note. An Irish car ferry slipped across the bay, pitching heavily. Sump-oil fires burning in great black drums sent thick clouds of smoke over where Evan's friend, Colin Priddey, moored his boat in the inner harbour.

On the end of a ten-yard jetty, Colin's thirty-foot motor vessel, *Athene*, rolled on the wash of an incoming cruiser, its car tyres strapped to the hull groaning against the quay. The perspex windows were so scratched, he couldn't see if Colin was aboard or not. It was an old boat, poorly maintained, and in the two years his friend had lived in it, Evan had never known him to take it out onto the open sea.

Evan swung the bike and Terence onto the deck. The hatch was unlocked and Evan climbed down backwards into the wheelhouse, coaching Terence to follow after him. From the wheelhouse another set of steps led into a galley. The galley was equipped with a sink, cooker and a table that converted into a double berth. The walls were varnished plywood, from which hung, among other things, paintings of a fox, M/V *Athene* and an eighteenth-century naval battle. Terence slid along a bench seat and rested his hands on the table.

'Doesn't look as if Colin's here, does it? Would you like something to eat?'

'What is there to eat?'

'Let's see what he's got, shall we?' His friend kept a tight ship, at least in the galley. Each mug had its hook and every plate was strapped down with elastic bungies. Sugar, tea and coffee were stored in sealed jars. A neat discipline was imposed everywhere, but nothing looked clean. The shelves were scored with grease and dust, the sink hadn't been scoured in months and Evan's shoes stuck to the cork floor. He ransacked the cupboard and the tiny fridge below it.

Within minutes he was putting lunch together: fried eggs, fried onions, tinned carrots, black sausage, half a pork pie, which he donated to Terence, and instant mashed potato. Evan placed the two plates down and sat across the table from Terence. Terence rested his head in one hand, his elbow on the table, and stabbed with his fork, sending the carrots skidding off the plate onto the floor. Evan bent down and picked the carrots off the carpet, blew off the dust before replacing them on Terence's plate. Terence tried to lift the egg whole from his plate, but it kept slipping off his fork. He laid down the fork and picked up the egg by its crisp black edge and hovered it over his mouth. He managed to get a few bites out of the egg before pointing to his plate.

'What is that?'

'That's black sausage.'

'What's black sausage?'

'Pig's blood.'

'I'm not eating that.'

'Right you are then, I'll have it.' After Evan had finished the black sausage and the rest of his meal, he sat back against the hull of the boat and eyed Terence's plate greedily. 'You don't have to eat the pork pie.'

'I will eat it.'

'But you don't have to, old man.'

'I'm saving it till last.'

'Terence, I think I should tell you. I spilt some pig's blood on it.'

Terence stared at his plate contemplatively. Finally he said, 'I don't want the pork pie,' with an air of sadness in his voice.

'Right you are .... I'll have it.' Evan stuck in his fork and excavated the pork pie.

While Evan waited for Terence to finish all he dared eat, he lit up a cigarette. With the same match he burnt the hairs growing thickly in his nostrils. The walls in Colin's galley were covered in military paraphernalia. Embroidered paratrooper wings pressed behind glass. A maroon beret hung from a nail on the wall. Bellerophon astride Pegasus in a gilt frame. A photograph of a parachute drop snapped from the cockpit of a Dakota C47. Evan looked away from all these trophies. He did not want to see them.

'That dinner tasted like a rat ran across it,' Terence said. Evan failed to respond. He picked up the plates, placing them into the aluminium sink. He didn't know how to get water to run in the boat and so left them there. He took out a tub of ice cream from the fridge. There was no freezer compartment and the ice cream had melted into a purée. He poured out the contents into two bowls. Evan saw a bottle of rum above the draining board and added a measure to one bowl. 'Have you any wafers?' Terence asked as he saw the ice cream for the first time.

'No.'

'Well Mummy always has wafers.'

'Think on it as a change, Terence.'

Terence whisked his ice cream with a spoon and Evan found himself copying him.

Evan walked through the boat, exploring. Terence kept ramming him from behind like a goat and grabbing his leg. Evan dropped across him finally, pinned his arms to the floor and kissed his nose zestfully. Evan let him get up when he realised he might bring back his lunch. 'Is this how you punch?' Terence clenched his fists and began jabbing.

'No, now stop it, Terence. My father put boxing gloves on me, Terence. I don't want you getting involved in that. Stop it! – He told me I'd make friends in the gym – Stop it, Terence. Say you love me instead.'

'No.'

'Why? Don't you love me?'

'Yes.'

'Well say it then.'

'I looww you.'

'Say it properly.'

'Don't want to.'

'Try saying . . . I hate you.'

'I hate you.'

'Ah, now that's easier to say, isn't it, Terence. But why? You don't hate me, do you? Terence listen to me. Those friends I made in the gym? Well, we punched the living Jesus out of one another.' Terence ignored his father's salutary warning and went in for another assault. As a last resort, Evan hung him by his trousers upside down from a hook on the back of the bedroom cabin door. Evan swung the door shut as he stepped into the wheelhouse. 'Don't let the rat bite you in there, Terence.'

Terence screamed so loudly, Evan rushed back into the bedroom and took the boy down. These boats were made of plywood. A scream like that could travel across the harbour.

Evan had the boy in his arms, crying for the third time that day, as a man came down the steps into the wheelhouse. He looked like a solvent for Terence's troubles, dressed as he was in a royal blue ambulance service uniform. It was Colin Priddey.

They hadn't seen one another for a year and Evan familiarised himself with Colin's appearance. Both men were in their late twenties, but whereas Evan's face was clouded, changing colour and texture every few minutes, recent experience seemed to have softened and relaxed Colin's countenance like a good moisturising cream. In his medic's uniform, Colin looked like the safest man on board. If ever I get shot, blown up or run down by a car, Evan thought, Colin would be the first man I would want to see.

Terence had stopped crying with Colin's arrival. His hold on Evan had changed from one of combat into an embrace, his father being now his only ally against the stranger. 'The kid's grown,' Colin said, inspecting Terence closely.

'You should see him standing up.'

'How old are you now?'

'Four,' Evan offered.

'No I'm not, I'm five,' Terence rectified.

'You don't remember me, do you, Terence?' Colin asked.

20

'Of course he doesn't remember you.'

'Shut up, Evan. I'm making conversation with the boy. Let him speak for himself.' Colin spun his cap onto a hook and climbed down into the galley.

They ended up around the table, Colin and Evan facing each other, Evan's big serpentine figure writhing, shifting on the seat, the cumbersome weight of his hands, like clubs, resting on the table top.

'Well, Terence, tell me . . . what are you interested in?' Colin asked.

Terence took a little time to reply. 'Superman. Going to Ashley's.'

'Who's Ashley?'

'He's my friend from school.'

'And what's that medal for, around your neck, Terence. Bravery?' Colin lifted the gold-coloured medal that hung on a blue string to see what was written there. But Terence told him anyway.

'I won it for ballet,' Terence announced.

Colin and Evan looked at one another perplexed. Neither really knew how to respond. Evan felt that it shouldn't be mentioned again, to avoid embarrassing the boy. But Colin was on another train of thought. 'You must be good at it then,' he said.

'I know my first position, second position, third position . . . that's all we've learnt so far.'

'Would you like me to make a cake?' Colin suddenly surprised them.

21

Evan looked puzzled. 'It's not his birthday.'

Colin noticed the dishes in the sink. 'Looks like you've eaten anyway.'

'We have.'

'Good. Well, I've just finished a shift and I'm ready for a drink more than anything else.'

'It's only 10 am,' Evan informed him.

'I've been working all night. You like a drink when you finish work, don't you? Since when have you been bothered about the time when a drink is being discussed, anyhow.'

'I'm thinking about the boy here,' Evan said distractedly, fiddling with a car radio embedded in the plywood wall, tuning into police communications on short wave.

'We can go and buy some drink and have it on the beach. He can play in the sand.'

'Good idea.'

'Let's go then.'

'Don't you want to change into mufti first, Colin?'

'No.'

They followed Colin out of the harbour basin and into the town, up narrow avenues of garish yellow pensions and houses, dead leaves and milk bottles on the doorsteps. Evan looked through every window, squinting as if the glass might explode in his face. He felt a deep suspicion of everything and everybody and scanned the rooftops, behind each

22

hedge and garden wall, panning to the right and to the left. He scrutinised young and old, people on their way to the shops, walking their dogs, waiting for buses. He marched in step with Colin and kept as close to the walls as he could, neglecting Terence, who had to run to keep up, and who was saying in one long breathless catharsis: 'I went to the dentist on Monday with Mummy and I didn't have to have one tooth taken out. He gave Mummy an electric toothbrush. One of my teeth fell out in the front when I was with Ashley. A new tooth pushed it out. That's what the dentist said it did. My friend Sam Bates has got teeth growing all over the place . . .'

It didn't help that Colin kept bumping into people, who he claimed were all women. 'Damn women. Pampered swine. You try walking in a straight line in this town. Impossible. You bump into women. Every time. They just come at you and expect you to do all the detours.'

The sight of a young woman smacking the bare legs of her tiny son because he had wandered off too far along the pavement inflamed him further. Colin broke step to give her a short sharp shock of his own. 'Approve of your children, Madam!' he yelled like a sergeant major. The woman stared at his uniform, at Terence standing to attention between the two men, and marched her child into a shop as quickly as she

could. 'These women who abuse their privileges . . .'
Colin said into the air.

Colin led them into a grocery store near the seafront. He bought two pints of vodka and a tube of
Smarties for the boy. After they cleared the inarticu-
late busy-ness of the town they set up on the sand,
the streets rippling behind their backs.

Terence ran to the edge of the sea and began walking
along a sewage pipe jutting into the sea. He got his feet
wet from the small waves that swept the pipe every
few seconds. The pipe was covered in a slimy green
seaweed. The water, about four feet deep on either
side, seemed to gurgle his name. Evan broke open
a bottle and put his head down beneath it for half
a minute. When he finally surfaced for air a third
of the bottle had gone. Colin watched in admiration
before taking a hit from the other pint. The wind
swept off the sea, slapping Evan in the face, like a
rebuke for drinking so early in the morning. His eyes
watered. 'Hell of a storm on Thursday,' Evan barked.
'Look what it did to the pier.'

'That pier had been up there a hundred years,' Colin
said. 'What were you doing during the storm?'

'Sailing over from Ireland.'

'You can't sail.'

'I can now.' Evan laughed.

Colin laughed too, without being intimate with
the reason. Evan gave his bottle of vodka another

work-out, then pointed to the sea. 'Have you taken your boat out there yet?'

'No and I never will. Everything I own in the world is on that boat. We should have brought some glasses with us. And some ice as well. That boat is never going to leave the harbour.'

'Do you mind if I use your place, your boat, as HQ for a while?' Evan asked.

'What's mine is yours. The kid as well?'

'Yeah.'

'Does his mother . . .'

'No she doesn't.'

'You should call her. Just to tell her.'

'I asked for your boat, not your advice,' Evan snapped, then sank the neck of the bottle into his mouth. The way he drank, rolled his eyes back, dug his feet into the sand, was like some kind of mountain animal. 'Celia is out of the picture. It's just me and the boy.'

'You can care for him, I suppose?'

'What's that meant to mean?'

'You have to do more than feed and water these little people.'

'I know that.'

'Why isn't he in school?'

'Because I took him out of school.'

'Without Celia's permission?'

'Why do I need her permission?'

'She's going to kill you.'

'How do you know that, Colin?' Evan twisted himself around to face him.

'From what you told me. She's a passionate woman.'

'She was jealous of you, old man.' Evan took a drink.

'There were things we told each other that you kept secret from her. I got all the keys to your mysteries, Evan. God help me. I even saved your life once.'

'And I saved yours.'

'What wife can compete with that? Of course Celia was fucking jealous.'

'I feel like part of your webbing equipment – that's what she said to me once.'

'That's a pretty vital part.'

'Like an appendage to my life. I think that's what she meant.'

'It's one thing to see these things, isn't it. Quite another to change them.'

Evan went quiet with his mouth clamped around the bottle neck. As he drank, he considered why he had never told her anything significant about his army experience. It was sensible in a perverse sort of way. How could you expect your spouse to keep up her love, if, when she asked, 'What did you do at work today, dear?' you replied, 'I shot a woman as she was giving birth.'

'When do you have to get back to your unit?' Colin asked.

'I'm not going back.'

'They'll come and get you. Sooner or later.'

'I'll face that when it comes.' Evan raised the bottle to his lips. The strength of liquor was an infusion of courage. He could feel it flushing around in his blood. He lit a cigarette and lay back, relaxing in the company of his three best friends. Colin, alcohol and tobacco. The boy was another thing. Terence was his flesh and blood. But this did not help him know what to do with him. It was a worrying thought, which Evan tried to conquer with another shot of vodka. A speeding fire engine passed along the seafront, its sirens blaring. Evan mimicked the sound in his throat, 'Hee-haw, hee-haw, hee-haw', and all his tension slid out along his tongue into the open air.

Terence, assuming his father was starting a game, picked it up from there. 'Hee-haw, hee-haw,' he said in a soprano voice.

'Don't you ever live out of uniform?' Evan turned on Colin, pulling at his NATO ambulance service sweater.

'People treat this uniform with respect. I'm a paramedic now, not a paratrooper.'

'Never vulnerable in a uniform, right?' Evan drifted a few feet away from Colin and Terence and lay on his back in the cold sand. Stars ran out into the morning sky. Brittle crashes of machinery and sharp-edged visuals everywhere softened kindly. He began to flush out memories. Such as the holiday by the sea he and his wife and Terence had taken further up the coastline. Evan's elbow had begun to bleed heavily on the beach which made Terence cry. 'You bleed more easily when you get older,' he told him, to allay his fears. Later that afternoon his wife attempted to dress his wound and discovered an old scar on his elbow had opened up. She prodded the skin tissue around the scar and said, 'Evan, you've got something in there.' She sterilised a pair of hairdressing scissors and rolled up the sleeve of his shirt into a tourniquet across his bicep. A clean sharp arrow of pain bolted through his arm into his head as she made an incision and removed a piece of glass shrapnel the size of a thumbnail. She held it up like a trophy smeared in blood.

Evan sat up in the sand to meet this image head-on and there was Terence at his feet, building a sandcastle. 'Will you help me?' he was asking.

Colin tipped forward on his knees, smiling, and began shovelling handfuls of sand into a pile. 'We have to make some parapets, observation posts, barbed wire out of seaweed . . . Evan, how do you build a sandcastle?' Evan did not answer. He was staring out to sea. Colin flattened the mound of sand and sculptured four towers, one at each corner.

He scraped out a moat and lined the bottom with pebbles. Terence sat on his haunches watching the castle take shape.

Colin detailed Terence to burrow a tunnel under the castle. Evan noticed and said, 'I never knew why you do that. Why do you need a tunnel under a castle?'

'I don't know. Let the water from the moat into the castle in times of siege. I dunno. But now we need water.'

'Can I get the water?' Terence had his hand up.

'Give him your bottle, Evan.'

'There's still some vodka in it.' Evan held the bottle up to see the state of play. He was about to drain the rest and pass over the bottle, when Terence accidently collapsed the castle tunnelling through.

'Oh no!' Terence said.

'Let's go for a walk.' Evan lifted Terence to his feet and led the way towards the bellying cliffs.

Colin and Evan, with Terence on his shoulders, walked around the footpath under the cliff, away from the town. Evan hurled his bottle into the sea. Then he started singing. Evan had a fair tenor voice, vandalised momentarily by cigarettes and booze. But as a rule his voice was good enough to have made him a living. He could give a fair hearing to *Linden Lea, The Old House, Terence's Farewell to Kathleen, Passing By, She Moved Thro the Fair.* All songs he'd learnt off John McCormack recordings. Evan had developed quite an obsession with the Irish tenor, especially his sentimental songs. McCormack's voice was more suited to Irish ballads than to opera. His strength being – he never patronised a simple lyric. On a line such as 'I did but see her passing by and yet I love her till I die' he sang without condescension or cynicism, harnessing all his classical training to lend truth to a sentiment. All the crap songs about Terence and Kathleen and Mother McCrea, Evan believed in when McCormack was singing.

'That's nice,' Colin complimented when Evan was finished.

'You should hear John McCormack sing it. He sings to our condition.'

'What is our condition?' Colin asked.

Evan searched for, but failed to find, an answer. He snatched Colin's bottle instead.

Cut into the rock fifty yards away and projecting into the sea was a fortress-style construction. Its wall was mounted by a wire fence with broken spotlights on every post. Evan swung Terence onto the ground, who ran ahead on reconnaissance. In the wall facing the path was a ticket booth painted in candy stripes, red and white and smeared with graffiti. SONS OF OWAIN GLYNDWR was carved into the wood. Evan helped his son over the turnstile and vaulted in after him, landing square on two feet. Colin's leap was less expert. His mouth burst open as he landed and the impact left him trembling.

Inside was an open-air swimming pool, a long time derelict, filled with rocks and piles of earth. An unmanned bulldozer sat idly on top of one of the piles. Surrounding the pool were stone tiers, where sunbathers had once cooked in the sun. The wind kept scouring layers of dust out of the pool into grey clouds. Evan walked around the rim of the pool looking over the edge, identifying used condoms, doll-heads, lager cans congealed in the mud. He felt dizzy suddenly and keeled over onto the stone tier. From where he fell, Evan watched Terence climb down into the pool and Colin balance along the edge with his arms outstretched. A mesh of hot wires fizzled in his head and his stomach burned with alcohol, making him nauseous and depressed. He just wanted to lie down somewhere, somewhere with cover, not the open-air pool. He stood up determinedly, only to fall down abruptly again, with his legs in the air, half blinded by tears, dust and vague violent mirages.

Colin came away from the edge of the pool and ran up the stone tiers towards Evan. For a moment Evan thought Colin meant to attack him, and he braced himself for an assault. But Colin was only after the vodka. He prised the bottle out of Evan's hand and tipped it back to his mouth. He wiped his mouth with his sleeve. 'What you going to do, then?'

'About what?'

'Your future, Evan.'

'I don't know what I'm going to do.'

'Maybe they'll forget about you. I knew a guy once who stayed AWOL for two years before they came and got him.'

'Not from the Provinces?'

'No, not from the Provinces.'

Terence came back from his adventure down in the pool, butting past Colin to sit by his father's side on the step.

'I should know what I'm going to do, shouldn't I?' Evan continued. 'Ten years in the army has taught me nothing.'

'It's not meant to. On the contrary.'

'What's that mean?'

'The army programmes you. It doesn't teach you initiative. Remember when we got into the Paras? Doing basic training with the Marines?'

'No.'

'Yes you do. We had to go onto a landing craft with a Marines CO, remember? When we got to the beach, the ramp went down and the CO shouted, "Disembark." But nobody moved. We just sat there until someone said, "Sir, we go by a different order in the Paras." "What order's that?" he asked. "Go, sir." "Go?" "Yes, sir. Go, sir." He thought it over for a moment, then yelled, "Go! Go! Go!" and all the paras leapt out instinctively from the landing craft onto the beach, like it was an aircraft.' Colin turned to address the boy. 'That's how dumb the army makes you, Terence. Me and your dad, we know. We were there in that landing craft together. But I'm out of it now. I'm cured of all that bullshit. I'm fucking cured!'

Colin raised the bottle as if to toast the fact, before running down the stone tiers with the bottle, nearly falling into the pool at the six-foot marker. Evan watched him carefully making his way to the diving boards while keeping an eye on Terence, down inside the pool again, filling an orange sack with coke cans, a milk carton, a piece of plastic dustbin, blue plastic netting, swinging the sack over his shoulder between each haul. He dragged out his cigarettes, lit one and dropped the lighted match into a puddle of water at his feet. The smoke took the edge off his nausea. Colin reached the top of the ladder and walked to the end of the diving board. He drained the bottle and threw it into the pool, where it smashed against a stone. Colin laughed, swayed in the wind, the crust of his chestnut hair sweeping across his face. A cloud of dust drifted beneath him. Evan shivered and the cigarette dropped from his fingers into the puddle of water with a hiss.

'Go!' Evan shouted. 'Go! Go! Go!'

Colin sprung off the diving board, his hands grasping above his head for harness straps that weren't there. For a moment he seemed to be suspended in mid-air, as if he really did have a parachute easing him down. With elbows in, toes up and legs squeezed tightly together and bent at the knees, Colin dropped through the cloud of dust until his feet smacked down on the floor of the pool. A pair of white mud wings spread out from under his feet, before Colin automatically curled into a landing roll. He leapt from the ground, his ambulance uniform covered in mud.

'Damn you, Price!'

'You ain't cured,' Evan said.

THREE

'Ball room, old man. Ball room.'

In the aft cabin Terence crouched in a zinc tub which Evan filled with water, warmed over the stove in a kettle. Evan plunged an arm in the water to force his legs open and free his testicles. With Terence comfortable, Evan could himself relax. He splashed the warm water around carelessly, descending into a trance until his eyes registered nothing but steam. He could hear Terence puffing with determination as he rubbed soap into his hair. Water splashing down his shirt brought Evan around again. He looked passionately at the wet orb that was Terence's head, at his long golden hair, tipped-up nose and eager young wrists guiding a toothbrush around his chest.

This was the first time Evan had given his son a

bath. He wouldn't have thought of it, had Terence not mentioned it was one of his routines. And only now did he understand what he'd been missing. He felt high, as though he were on some soft little drug. He could feel the hair rising on the back of his neck and a sensual lightheadedness. To feel as easy as this, Evan usually had to go fifty lengths in a swimming pool after lifting weights for two hours. This was some work-out, he thought.

Evan pulled him out of the water and draped him in a towel. The water ran down Terence's legs and formed glistening spheres on his square feet. His features were miniatures, that was how Evan saw them. His son's nose, button mouth, chin like a bent hairpin – were miniatures that would become big one day. A little fragile thing, three and a half feet off the ground. That was all Evan really knew about his son. And that he had won a ballet medal which hung from his neck.

Terence broke away from his father, climbed onto the bed and bounced up and down on his feet. 'Can I have a drink?' he said.

Evan wanted to play a game first. 'Only if your name is Dracula can you have a drink.'

'My name is Dracula,' Terence obliged.

Evan left him using the bed as a trampoline and fetched a glass of milk from the galley. 'Here you are, Dracula,' he said upon returning. 'Drink it up.'

Terence emptied the glass and handed it back. He just managed to blurt out, 'My name's not Dracula, it's Terence,' before cracking up.

Evan liked this game, because it had made his son laugh. 'What! Come here . . .' Evan dived on the bed and gave Terence an ankle tap. The boy bounced once on his back and onto the floor. A short silence was broken by a piercing scream. Evan's stomach contracted. He picked him off the floor, held him in his arms and felt his son's tears driving a course between their welded cheeks.

'You hurt Mummy too!'

'Terence, your mother makes mistakes as well.'

'I'll tell her you pushed me off the bed.'

'I didn't push you off. It was an accident.'

'You make Mummy cry. You frighten her sometimes and make her cry.'

'There, there, Terence,' Evan hummed, as much to calm himself as Terence. The deeper he got into childcare, the more stressful it became. 'There, there, old man. You stop crying and I'll tell you a story.'

Evan drew the curtains in the cabin, helped Terence get into the double bed and covered him in the quilt. Terence would not go to sleep unless Evan went to sleep beside him. Evan kicked off his shoes and lay down and began the story he'd promised.

'There was once a gypsy whose wife died and left him their son to raise. He and his father travelled all around the country and saw many sights together. He taught his son how to catch trout by tickling them under the belly and how to shoe horses. The boy never went to school. Then one day two men came to the gypsy's caravan in the forest and took away his son. They told the gypsy he could only have his son back when he found a house to live in. Now living in a house is not the way for gypsies. They are nomads. But this gypsy loved his son and so had no choice but to give up a way of life as natural to him as flying is to a bird. It is said that gypsies steal children. But this particular gypsy knew it was the other way around. After a couple of months, the gypsy made enough money to put down a deposit on a house and found a permanent job in a town. He went back to the men who had taken his son away and said, I now have a house. Can I have my son back please? But the men wouldn't let him have his son back, because they claimed he had settled in with a new family of foster parents, who could give him more than a gypsy, even if he did have a house. The gypsy abandoned the house he had bought and went away in his grief, howling like a wolf. So if ever you hear a wolf crying in the night, you'll know that that gypsy has passed through your town.'

'I don't like that story,' Terence sighed.

'Nor do I really.'

'I know what an eyas is.'

'What is it?'

'It's a young hawk stolen from its nest.'

'You know lots of things, don't you, Terence.'

'My teacher told me at school. Mrs Benson knows everything about hawks. Can I have another drink?'

'A small one.'

Evan took Terence's empty glass and returned it to the galley. He half filled it with milk from the fridge. The chilled glass burned in his hand like a chalice. As Evan went back to the aft cabin he found Terence sitting up in bed, clutching his 9mm Browning pistol.

'Terence, give me that, please,' he said coldly.

'Is it a real gun?'

'Yes.'

'Whose is it?'

'Army issue.' Evan retrieved the pistol, checked the safety and put it back into his inside jacket pocket. He hung the jacket from a hook in Colin's wardrobe and shut the door. Then he lay down next to Terence.

'I wish I had a real gun.'

'A toy gun's better.'

'But I've already got a toy gun.'

'I can't swap you, old man. Guns aren't all they're cracked up to be. You've got a bike. Now that's much more fun.'

'It's too big for me, though. Can I see the gun again?'

'No.'

'Please. Just once.'

39

'No, Terence. In fact, I'd appreciate if you could try and forget you ever saw it the first time. You know, blast it right out of your mind. You mustn't tell anyone you've seen a real gun, or I'll be in real shit. Do you understand? It's our secret, right?'

'Okay.'

'Good boy.'

'I would still like a real gun, though.'

'Oh Christ. Go to sleep, please, and in the morning I'll buy you a penknife.'

They lay side by side for five minutes in silence. Evan chanced a furtive glance to see if Terence had dropped off.

The boy was wide awake. 'Last Christmas I felt this sort of tickling in my feet. And there was hot breath in my face. I didn't open my eyes once. Next Christmas I'm going to keep one eye open like this . . .' Terence demonstrated holding his eyelid open with his fingers.

'I wouldn't do that if I were you.'

Terence shifted around, whistled through the gap in his front teeth, pretended a couple of times to be asleep, until he eventually dropped off. Evan watched him in his sleep, listening to the rhythm of his breathing, listening to the air darken. He lightly brushed the boy's cheek with the back of his fingers.

Evan told himself he was not a cruel father, only an inadequate one, unprepared. In his world, all men are amateur parents, if they are lucky enough to get to play parent at all. In Evan's world the men went to war while the women raised the children single-handed. These rigid and unyielding boundaries were peculiar to Aldershot, home of the army, a strange and tenebrous town where intense outbursts of domestic strife were quotidian and the threat of violence permanently hung in the air. It was not a wholesome environment in which to bring up children. No squaddies' town ever could be. He found himself conceding some ground to Celia. She had been right to insist they move from there several years ago, and live among civilians. At the time he saw no advantages in moving, just the inconvenience of having to commute to work.

Evan rolled off the bed and picked up his jacket from the wardrobe. He closed the bedroom door gently behind him, tip-toed across the wheelhouse and clambered down into the galley. He drew the curtains in the galley, took out the Browning and put it on the table in front of him. He removed the magazine and drew back the slide to empty the chamber, then replaced the round in the magazine. He pushed his finger into the clip, depressing the rounds against the spring at the bottom. The clip had eleven rounds left out of a maximum thirteen. He stripped the weapon down, cleaned each part with a dry tea towel and reassembled it in ten minutes. The close-quarter weapon was so neat and petite he could almost conceal it in the palm of his hand. Evan raised the pistol to his head. All that mattered in the world now was his son. The army could go to hell. That was what he kept thinking, over and over.

The issue was more complex in actual fact, he had to accept. The moment he put the pistol down on the table, he didn't know what really mattered any more. All he knew was what he *didn't* want. He didn't want to be in the Services any longer.

He had to take each day as it came, manoeuvring away from where he'd recently been, navigating into his future by dead reckoning, walking backwards like a squaddy on the Ardoyne Road. With the pistol in his trouser pocket, Evan stepped out of the boat onto the jetty. It was almost dark as he walked through the harbour, the rigging tapping out a neurotic melody on aluminium masts. At the end of the harbour wall was a small unmanned lighthouse. Using a piece of limestone, Evan scratched a rectangle onto the wooden door. He paced out ten metres and reached for the weapon. Evan thumbed off the safety and held the pistol in an extended hand, supported underneath by his left palm. He squeezed off four sensational rounds into the lighthouse door. Discharging the rounds left him feeling giddy, as though reunited with an old love. Evan walked over and inspected the target. He found the group wide and the mean point of impact high of the rectangle. Evan zeroed the pistol, adjusting the foresight up one notch, from 3 to 4. As he walked back again to aim, he spotted a group of animated people walking in his direction along the harbour wall. He flicked on the safety catch and dropped the pistol back into his pocket. He passed the group of teenage boys with his head bowed and eyes rolled into his skull.

He had intended to discharge all eleven rounds before the teenagers disturbed him. Evan believed in what Chekhov had written somewhere, that if a gun appears in the first act, sometime during the course of the play that gun has to be used. Evan could not quite bring himself to part with the pistol, but he was content to discharge the live ammunition. It seemed a fair compromise.

He returned to the boat. Colin was still at work and would be until morning. He found a book in the boat on World War II and read about the Parachute Regiment's campaign in Arnhem. At eleven he fell asleep at the table, but by midnight was pacing around the tiny spaces in the boat. He had not yet got used to sleeping more than a couple of hours at a time. To work off his insomnia he tried polishing his boots with spit. Then he cleared a space in the wheelhouse and got down on the floor to do some press-ups. There was a time when he could manage a hundred press-ups with a thirty-pound Bergen rucksack on his back. But without the motivation of a forthcoming mission, all Evan could manage was fifty unladen.

At 5 am, still unable to sleep, he stripped off his clothes and stood naked in front of a full-length mirror behind a door, straining to see beyond himself, far into the distance beyond the image, to an Eden of non-conscious delights. At 7 am he cracked open a fresh bottle of vodka and within an hour was half way down it. When Colin returned, carrying fresh bread and milk in his cap, Evan was curled up in the wheelhouse, clutching the empty bottle, snoring, without a stitch of clothing to cover himself.

FOUR

On the Monday morning Colin came back from work with an American edition of Monopoly he'd found in a charity shop. In the afternoon, when he had slept a few hours, the three of them sat around the table playing. It was a moody, bad tempered game. Colin had bought the set with an eye to entertaining the boy. But it was too sophisticated for the five-year-old and Terence was only marginally engaged, throwing the dice for all players. So it all seemed a waste of time to Evan, who didn't have the patience for such things anyway. Thirty minutes into the game, Colin owned all the real estate around the gaol and Evan, with diminished resources, was laying all his hopes on the chance to buy Broadwalk to clinch that corner of the market. Then Evan landed on one of Colin's properties covered with houses and

45

had to part with $800 rent. He decided to sell a few railways back to the bank.

'You can't sell them,' Colin stopped him.

'Who says?'

'The rules say.'

'Where does it say that? There aren't any rules in this box.'

'You have to mortgage your properties if you want to borrow money.'

'I don't want to mortgage them. I don't *want* them any more. I want to sell them.'

'You can't.'

'Don't be stupid.'

'It's not stupid.'

'You can do that in real life.'

'This is not real life.'

'No shit!' Evan snatched up his cigarettes.

'It's a game, Evan. You're meant to have fun playing games.'

'Well I don't.' Evan tossed his money at Colin. 'Have it all.'

Terence pressed himself into the wall opposite Evan, swinging his legs, kicking the table support with his feet. He looked blanched and his eyes glazed over with intensities. 'You're frightening Terence,' Colin advised in a whisper.

'Now you sound like his mother.'

Colin shook his head and stacked his counterfeit

money a little more neatly. Terence laid his hands on the table, palms up, and Colin smacked them, thereby beginning another game within the game, in which Terence withdrew his hands several times before Colin could slap them. They were all laughing except for Evan. Colin turned his hands over for Terence. Terence raised his arm above his head and plunged downwards. Colin withdrew his hands. Terence followed through and fell off his seat. Evan was amazed to suddenly see the boy inverted, his toes hooked onto the edge of the bench, holding himself against the floor with his hands. How could a game end like that, upside down? Children, Evan thought admiringly . . . whatever they do, they give it their all. That was the spirit of the Airborne Regiment. Evan gripped a piece of Terence's sweater and hauled him back onto the seat.

Evan lit up a cigarette and topped up his cold coffee with Puerto Rican rum. He stared at Colin staring at him, then turned his head to the window, bringing the cigarette and coffee mug to his mouth alternately.

'You know what my favourite part is, in the Carnival of the Animals? It's the bit at the end,' Terence said.

'Carnival of the Animals – is that a book?' asked Colin.

'It's a tune by Saint-Saëns.'

'What happens in the end.'

47

'The animals all play their instruments together.'

'Cultured little chap, isn't he,' Colin smiled. But Evan wasn't paying attention. There was something interesting in the harbour. A black Vauxhall Cavalier parked near the chandlers' arches, registration number 35 KG 75. Terence threw the dice for Evan, getting a five and a three score. He counted the numbers on his fingers, then moved Evan's battleship eight places onto Broadwalk.

'Daddy! Daddy! You've landed on Broadwalk.'

Evan held up his hand to silence the boy. He kept his hand to Terence's mouth and made a rapid survey of the area outside the boat. A sloop-rigged ketch was entering the inner harbour through the lock gates on its engines. 'Does your engine work on this boat?' Evan demanded.

'I don't know. I expect so,' Colin replied hastily, recognising an intelligence-gathering question.

'Are the batteries charged?'

'Yes.'

'But Daddy . . . you're on Broadwalk . . .' Evan did not respond as he slid out of the seat and climbed the steps. In the wheelhouse he dug around until he found what he wanted – the ignition keys on a hook – and inserted the biggest of the three keys into the ignition. Nothing happened as he turned the key. When he turned it the opposite way, anti-clockwise, the twenty-horsepower engine beneath his feet groaned into life. The sound conjured Colin out of the galley. 'What the hell you doing?'

'Untie the boat, Colin.'

'I'm not taking this boat out! You know I've never taken her off the mooring. Turn the engine off.'

'Untie the fucking ropes!' Evan silenced him. Colin did not come back a second time. He at last recognised what Evan was doing. He was giving him an order. Colin obeyed the Captain and went up on deck to free the ropes from the dollies.

Terence attempted to enter the wheelhouse and Evan snarled at him too. 'Get back in there and don't come out until I say.' The way Terence scrambled back down left Evan with a feeling of guilt. He didn't want to frighten the boy, reign by terror.

When Colin jumped onto the jetty he rocked the boat a little. Evan dug into his pocket for old faithful and laid it on the compass. Through the window he surveyed the middle distance, while Colin, in the corner of his eye, untied the ropes fore and aft and threw the coils up onto the deck.

Evan palmed the gear into reverse and began to back the boat out of its mooring. Once clear of the jetty he brought it around and headed down the channel, passing a dozen landings, heading for the lock. Colin appeared in the wheelhouse. 'Why are we moving?'

'The provost are in the harbour.'

'Who knows you're here?'

'I never told them.' Evan grinned, 'Did you?'

'They have good intelligence. Or good reason for wanting you.'

'They have good reason.' Evan steered *Athene* into the open inner gate of the lock, shunting the engine into reverse and forward to get the boat stationary. The harbour master's head appeared in the window of his control tower. Seconds later the gate rose out of the water behind them and the water level began to fall.

'I don't know what you did over there, but I guess it wasn't just . . .'

'It's the wrong time to talk about it now. Look . . .'

Evan pointed to where he had spotted two provost sergeants walking around the harbour perimeter on their starboard side. Both men were dressed in khaki, service dress number two. But it was their crimson arm bands and crimson sash around their caps that unequivocally gave them away.

When the provost started jogging towards the lock, Evan took his pistol off the compass and drew back the slide.

'That's a bit dramatic, isn't it?' Colin cautioned.

'No it's not.'

'Don't forget the boy.'

'You don't have to tell me about the boy. He's my son. I'll fight for him if I have to.'

The provost reached the end of the harbour wall

just as the outer gates were opening. Evan put the engine into gear and eased her out. The width of the harbour mouth was seventy feet and Evan could see their faces tumefying with anger, as they caught their breath under the control tower. The MP with the pork-chop sideburns and moustache punched his colleague in the arm and the two men began to run back to where they had parked their Cavalier.

'How far do you want to go?' Colin asked, as they left the outer harbour, looking nervously into a greater expanse of water than he'd ever seen before through the windows of his boat.

'We'll have to put in somewhere where the road doesn't reach. You know a place like that?'

'Pwlldu.'

'Where's that?'

'About three miles west along the coastline.'

'That'll do. Can we be seen putting in from the headland?'

'I don't know.'

'I can always sail her to Southern Ireland. England doesn't have an extradition treaty with Ireland.'

'Listen . . . Evan . . . this boat has no VHF or radar. I don't know the port from the starboard. It may be taking in water now for all we know. And I can't swim.'

'You can't swim?'

'Well, not properly.'

'Okay. We'll stick to the first plan.'

'Everything I own . . .'

'Is on this boat . . . I know,' Evan finished for him. 'Don't worry. If she starts to sink I'll gun her straight for shore and ground her on the beach.'

Colin sighed and looked across the bow into the azure sky at the escort of gulls, ducking and diving overhead.

The two men said very little to each other for the next thirty minutes, as Evan navigated as close to the coastline as possible. They passed the derelict swimming pool in the sea wall. From this angle it reminded Evan of the 'fort' on the Crumlin Road, also dressed in spotlights and barbed wire, and to where he and Colin had been posted in 1983. Evan would take his section out to patrol the area and Colin's section would give cover from the observation posts in the fort. On the next day they'd change roles.

Now he and Colin were working together again, and it felt very natural to both men.

Evan was keeping so close to the cover of the heather-clad cliffs rising out of the sea that they disturbed a flock of young surfers, sitting on their boards where the waves broke over a sand-bar. The swells passed beneath the hull, rattling the crockery in the galley, and hollowed out over the sand-bar. The surfers picked up the waves, appearing in gravity-defying positions from behind the crest.

The next bay was Pwlldu. Evan motored in as close as possible, decreasing the engine revs, throwing her into neutral. He ducked into the galley where he found Terence sitting at the table surrounded by Monopoly dollars. 'We're leaving the boat, Terence.'

'Where we going?'

'On an exercise.'

'What exercise?'

'Wait and see.'

Evan opened up several cabinets until he found a suitable canvas hold-all bag. Inside was a flare gun and four cartridges. Not so unprepared, Colin. Evan tipped the contents onto the floor. Into the bag he dropped his pistol, a penknife from the drawer, a lump of cheese and a carton of orange juice from the fridge, Terence's duffel coat and a towel. He wanted more food, a waterproof sheet, some basic tools and a shovel, but hadn't the time to look. Evan picked up his son like a rugby ball under his arm and climbed into the wheelhouse.

'Take the boat in slowly close to those rocks,' he instructed Colin. 'The water will be deep enough. It's high tide.' Evan thrust out his hand to Colin. For a moment the other man looked bewildered, unfamiliar with the protocol.

Then he grasped his friend's hand in his two hands.

'Take some of this.' Colin produced his wallet and plucked out all the paper money, a wad of ten-pound notes. Evan took the money and rolled it into his own back pocket.

Colin bent down to Terence – mute and floppy now on account of all the tense excitement – and kissed him on the cheek. Evan was staggered. He had never kissed his son like that. Colin made it all seem so easy, so natural.

Evan went forward with the boy, leaving Colin in the wheelhouse to bring the vessel in and make a fetch against the rocks. As Evan was looking for the right moment to jump off, Terence asked, 'Can I take my bike?'

'No, sorry, old man. We'll come back for it another day.'

'I wish I could take my bike.'

'I wish you could too. But as you say, it's too big anyway.'

'I don't care.'

'There won't be any good places for bikes where we're going.'

'Where are we going?'

'I don't know exactly. But there'll be hills.'

Evan spotted a good landing, a nice plateau of rock rising out of the sea, four feet off the port side. He threw the hold-all out of the boat onto the rock. With a foot planted on the gunwale, he lifted Terence over his shoulder, and as the hull grazed the rock, leapt off the boat. He landed on one foot and slipped on the seaweed straight onto his arse, fighting all the way down to save Terence from coming a cropper. Terence crawled out of the escapade without a scratch and even with a discernible smile.

'Well,' Evan sighed. 'We've broken the jinx, I think.'

Colin had turned the boat around and was already heading neurotically back home, with all his worldly possessions rattling around him. Evan got to his feet and began picking his way gingerly over the weed-clad rocks.

They had fifty metres of this dead ground to clear before the cover of sand-dunes and a path out of there. Terence wanted to look for crabs on the way. Evan knew that time was not working for them, that they had to be off that beach as soon as possible. But he also remembered how he had poleaxed his son with threats in the boat. He didn't want to alienate Terence any more and so compromised safety for Terence to indulge himself, and just hoped his interest would be short-lived.

Evan watched *Athene* diminishing on the pearl-grey sea as Terence scratched away with his fingernails at small rocks. He seemed rehearsed, seemed to know where to find them. He put his hands around a rock bigger than himself and tugged. 'Will you pick up this rock for me?'

'You think there's a crab under it?'

'There's got to be one under here. It's enormous!'

Evan got down to shift the rock. There were no crabs underneath, however, just snails and bloodsuckers, which he kicked off with his boot. 'No crabs here, Terence. And no more time to fool around. We're clean out of time.'

'But we haven't caught a crab yet.'

'Maybe there's none here. Have you considered that?'

'We haven't looked everywhere.' Terence carried on, kicking and lifting stones that were perched on the edge of rock pools without finding a single crab. 'You can usually find baby crabs,' Terence explained, with a hint of hysteria in his voice. In a final move of confidence he dropped to his knees beside a stone with a fringe of weed all around it. He rubbed his hands together before overturning the stone. Underneath was a medium-sized crab, black and motionless, relying on its camouflaged shell, now its cover had been blown.

Terence jumped to his feet screaming. His movement triggered the crab into a sideways getaway, making for the rock pool. Evan lifted his foot to crush it, but was stopped by Terence's plea. 'Don't kill it! I want to keep it.'

'How are we going to keep it? It's not a puppy dog, Terence. A crab needs water.'

'I want to keep it, just for a while.'

'For fuck's sake, Terence. You've found a crab. You never said anything about keeping one. Now let's go!'

Terence stamped his foot. 'I hate you!'

'No. Don't say that, please.'

'I hate you.'

'Please . . . I can't stand that.'

'Why won't you let me keep the crab?' Terence's lips had started quivering.

'Because it will die.'

'I'll look after it.'

Evan scanned the headland, the roofs of moving cars above hedgerows. He couldn't waste any more time. 'Okay. Keep it. You going to pick it up or am I?'

'It's getting away.'

Evan picked up the crab, keeping his fingers behind the claws. The crab was about four inches in diameter, frisky, with bright red eyes. Evan dropped it into the hold-all and drew back the zip.

'I'm going to call him George,' said Terence.

'That's nice,' said Evan. 'Let's hope we live longer than George is going to.'

FIVE

Evan Price met his wife in the Cambridge Military Hospital in Aldershot, where she was a staff nurse and he an appendicitis patient. She was very tough on her patients, he noticed, not least the terminal cases. When Evan confronted her with tongue in cheek about that, she told him she couldn't surrender to easy emotion and function properly. Evan found he could relate to that. He was in much the same line of business; fear being the emotion he daren't be intimate with. Nursing had made her hard-nosed, but not hard-hearted, she said, and called her brand of care 'tough love'.

Celia McAfee had contentious grey eyes framed by crow's-feet. Her red hair, too thick to grow out, was cut short every three months. She was taller than Evan

by one inch, and in trousers often seemed more like a
man than a man did.

They became lovers the day Evan was discharged
from hospital. It was only then Evan discovered she
was a lot of things besides a nurse. She played a
decent game of snooker and sang semi-professionally
around the working men's clubs in Hants. She could
move men to tears without them knowing why. But
Evan knew why. Celia's legacy was she killed her first
husband in a car crash, and her second husband had
never recovered from a mental breakdown. He was
festering in an asylum somewhere. All this sadness
travelled on her singing voice.

Once, before Evan met her, Celia got an audition with
the Royal Opera. They kept bringing her back, but finally
turned her down, ending her one and only quest to be
a professional singer on the grounds that she was too
antagonistic to work with. As the director put it, 'Your
voice is wonderful, but your personality's a disease.'

'My personality informs my voice, asshole. You
can't have one without the other,' she replied.

Celia didn't need a gun to kill. Although she did
learn how to fire Evan's weapons on the ranges. It
was her thrill to empty a whole clip of 7.62mm rounds
through an SLR, an event she always wanted to follow
by sex. She told him on numerous occasions that she
liked the fact he was a soldier. 'Perhaps you'll last
longer than the other two.'

Then Terence was born and she changed. Mothering mellowed her, tenderised her. She became fiercely protective of the boy and even gave up nursing to look after him. 'I don't want some fearful old nanny spanking him,' she would say. 'I'm not trusting him to someone else, someone like I used to be. Now you, Evan, are still the way you used to be. You've got the wrong instincts.' This was one of her first warnings.

By the time Terence reached three, Celia had forced them all to live outside of Aldershot. She wanted the boy isolated from the military world. Unfortunately for Evan, he was of that world. This he discovered to his cost on returning from a six-month tour in Belize. 'You can't come home for good, Evan. It won't work,' she told him within an hour of his arrival on British soil.

'Why not?' he asked, still smiling at that point.

'I've got used to a part-time marriage, I guess.'

'What about Terence?'

'The same. You're his part-time father.'

'And who decides all this?'

'Perhaps, if you bought yourself out of the army . . .'

'And do what? The only skill I've ever been taught since leaving school is soldiering.'

'Retrain for something. You're young enough.'

'I don't think so . . .'

'So you're going to stay in the army until they pension you off?'

'What's so bad about that?'

'Then you must stay in the garrison when you're not on tour.'

'What are you saying?'

'I don't want to live with you any more.'

'This is my house.'

'It's my home . . . until you turn up battle-scarred and heavy and start taking over. We don't like it, Evan.'

'We? Who is we?'

'Terence and me.'

'Perhaps you should let Terence speak for himself.'

'At four! He can't speak for himself. I am his voice until he gets older. I speak for him.'

'You're my wife, Celia,' Evan tried to bid.

'The army's your wife. I'm the bit on the side.'

Celia had reversed her attitude to soldiers. Pre-motherhood, soldiers had been sexy. Evan in camouflaged fatigues, webbing equipment, red beret used to make her blush with excitement. But now soldiers just made bad family men. Evan was up to his neck in a system that generated evil as a way of sustaining itself. He had gone out of fashion.

The regiment had a pastoral service and Evan went to speak with a counsellor there. Evan shared some cigarettes with the regimental counsellor and listened to him ask, 'When is your next tour, Captain?'

'I'm in Greenham Common for a couple of weeks. After that, Germany.'

'Good. Good. Just keep a low profile until you embark and you'll probably find when you get home from Germany she's so happy to see you, all this trouble will have blown over.'

'Do you think so?'

'Positive. This kind of problem occurs all the time. Long absences from the wife make her a little touchy. She'll come round. Take my word for it.'

When Evan returned from Germany, Celia told him that she wanted a divorce.

Evan lay down in a darkened room, vexed and ghosted. The Armed Services fight for the country when called upon to do so. Breaking that down into subjective units, each soldier was fighting to protect his family – his wife, children. If Celia divorced him, then he would have no one to fight for.

Then he remembered he still had a son. He walked downstairs where Celia was prowling like a cat and returned her fire. 'You can divorce me if you like, but no law can change my status as Terence's father.'

'Don't be sentimental, Evan. Since he was born you've seen him, what, six times a year? If that. When I was pregnant you were positively hostile to the idea of being a father.'

Evan had been on his first tour of duty in the Provinces throughout the last six months of Celia's pregnancy. This was late 1981, in the violent after-math of Bobby Sands's successful hunger strike in the Maze. Much of Evan's experience on that tour was of kids as young as four throwing stones and petrol bombs at him. Then in the thirty-ninth week of Celia's pregnancy a five-year-old IRA courier wan-dered into the barracks begging chewing gum. He left his school satchel behind, which exploded killing three of Evan's company. Eight hours later Evan was back in Aldershot with Celia, on compassionate leave. He couldn't touch her. He just looked at her swollen belly as she lay under a white sheet and thought how it looked like a burial mound. Celia sobbed every night into the pillow, her back turned against him. When the baby became overdue she refused to get out of bed at all. Evan laboured around the house for her, but said nothing from one day to the next. When Terence was induced two weeks late, she claimed he had exerted his will to deny the boy life. Evan never challenged this.

In the old days when there were just the two of them, living in the garrison's married quarters, Celia would finish her shift at the hospital, come home and go to work on him, massaging his tendons and muscles with Egyptian oil, laying cold compresses on ankles swollen from training exercises. Some days she'd even shave him, licking the blood off his chin where she nicked him with the razor. After

Terence was born Evan found himself competing for her favours.

Celia filed for divorce and an injunction was served on him at the garrison, preventing him seeing Terence until the divorce was settled. He drove straight to the house near Fleet in the middle of the night and banged on the door. There was no answer, but she was in there all right. You couldn't fool an old soldier. He punched a hole through the glass and twisted the lock open from inside. She was there all right, standing on the stairs in the darkness. 'You can't see him,' she said. 'Oh, yes I can . . .' Celia stepped across his path up the stairs. Suddenly there were only two sounds in the room. Evan slapping her and her hitting the floor. He found Terence in his bedroom, sitting rigidly up in bed, turning a torch on and off.

'Don't worry, son,' Evan petted him. 'Daddy's home, don't cry. There, there.'

Evan was in Northern Ireland, South Armagh, twenty-four hours after the incident, thereby dodging civil arrest.

That was the last time he saw Celia and Terence until Friday last, when he went to get Terence from the school. This time he broke no windows, slapped no women. He set up a covert OPS in a stolen car near the school and watched Terence snap off from his mother at the school gates at 0900 hours and walk tentatively through the mysterious dull thunder of the playground. The moment Celia was out of sight, Evan broke cover and waded in and found the boy among the many other children. 'We're going on holiday, old man.'

'Mummy said I wasn't to go off with you.'

'You're my flesh and blood . . .'

'There's blood on your hands.'

'Your mother coached you to say that, didn't she?'

Terence caught hold of Evan's right hand and raised it to show his father. Evan's knuckles were red raw. He had no memory of grazing them. Evan buried his hand into his pocket and ushered the boy towards the gate. A woman patrolling the playground materialised and blocked Evan's path. She put her large body into his way each time Evan tried to side-step around her. 'What game are *you* playing?' he asked finally.

'Where are you going with that boy?'

'He's my son.'

'How do I know that?' The woman bent over Terence. 'Is this your daddy, dear?'

Terence nodded. But he didn't appear entirely confident.

'Satisfied?' Evan growled.

'You can't take him off the premises unless you've informed the head.'

'Well, I've made my arrangements. Sorry I can't stop to chat. Bye-bye.'

'I'll check, if you don't mind. You wait here please.'

Evan did not like taking orders from a civilian woman and flushed hot and cold. He resented having to answer for himself like that to an anonymous babysitter who didn't even know Terence's name. He didn't for one second consider that she might have had Terence's interests at heart.

The woman kept looking back over her shoulder as she walked to the school entrance. She broke into a run on the final stretch. Evan made his move. 'Come on, Terence, we're leaving.'

They ran out of the playground to the parked car.

He drove west to South Wales. For Wales is a benign nation, a sanctuary. Except they didn't make it into Wales that day. A force ten gale had closed the Severn Bridge. Evan had to double back to find a small hotel near Bristol for the night. In the morning they abandoned the stolen car in the station and caught a train to complete the journey.

The motel was set off the road, five miles north of Pwlldu. It was deep into the night and Terence was asleep in one of the twin beds. As usual, Evan couldn't sleep longer than a cat's nap and was soon propped up against the bare lemon wall, working on a pint of scotch. Around 2 am he picked up the telephone in his room and got an outside line from the motel desk. He tapped out Celia's telephone number and slid down under the sheet with the receiver. When Celia breathlessly answered the telephone he couldn't stop himself trembling and all his words shook out of his reach. 'Hello,' she said. 'Hello . . . Evan . . . is that you?'

'Yes.'

'Evan . . . bring him back right now. Do you hear me? Right now, bring him back.'

'I can't do that right now.'

'Evan! Please! This feels like a death sentence.'

'To have your child taken away . . . yeah, I know.'

'Bring him back . . .'

Evan unloosed the speech he'd been composing for days. 'You shouldn't have tried to take him from ME! You've got to shoulder some of the blame for my actions here, Celia. Terence hasn't just got the one parent, he's got a father too. He wouldn't exist without me. I know there's more to it than that. But there's also more to it than nine months' pregnancy. I want to be a good father. With a little coaching I could have made it. But you had to play God didn't you. You never gave me a chance. You never gave Terence a chance either. What right had you to do that? Who is there with more authority than you to judge *your* mistakes . . . ?'

'Bring him to me, please.'

'You're not listening, are you?'

Celia began to sob. 'Bring him home,' she kept repeating, 'bring him home.'

'I can't. I'm only calling to tell you he's okay. He's happy. We're having a ball. I'm ringing off now.'

'No, please . . .'

Evan placed the receiver on the cradle and exhaled an awful lot of emotion. He reached for the whisky. He was drunk but not drunk enough. Evan unscrewed the cap and fed the spirit into his broken body.

Terence's head was pressed into the pillow, his hair matted and spiky. They didn't have a comb between them, nor a toothbrush. The room smelled of sweat, dirty socks and urine; the scent of their own decay, of hopelessness. It was surprising how it only took a couple of days before you started smelling like a vagrant.

He dropped off and came to an hour before dawn. The room was bathed in a blood-red glow. Terence was snoring in the other bed. Evan could not see anything clearly. He pushed against the mattress and fell off the bed onto the floor. He arched himself against the other bed frame where Terence lay. He wanted to see his boy. But the harder he squinted the less he saw. He knew he was in a motel room with Terence but what he felt actually surrounding him belied that description. The alcohol had taken him to an altitude no aircraft ever reached. He gripped the post of the bed and gazed through a cloud at a large gothic house. Then its door opened and a singing light stuttered sparks everywhere. The sparks exploded into children before his eyes, floating to earth under developing silk canopies. He cried as he witnessed their descent. By the time they had reached the ground, all the children had grown up into adults.

SIX

Evan sat in the rear of the empty bus, gripping the seat in front with both hands as the driver gunned into the head of the valley. Terence ran up and down the aisle, unrestricted by his father, who was preoccupied with his hangover and the landscape, not quite believing what he was seeing. They were driving through what used to be the most intensely mined valley in the world. This was The Valley and, on the day he had parted from there to enlist, was a black nexus of collieries, with hundreds of miners toing and froing along the streets. It had been very dramatic then. And so it came as a shock to see all those collieries closed down, the mine shafts plugged, slag tips sown with grass. One hundred years of industrial life had suddenly vanished. In every village whole terraces of miners' cottages lay abandoned, scrambling up the hillsides as if to escape the valley below. Like columns retreating after an arduous campaign.

In the last village in the valley the bus turned in the square, pointing its nose back down the hill. A group of colliers hunkered down together in the square, as though before a mirage of a coal seam. They gave Evan a cursory glance, in half recognition of one of their sons. Evan hadn't been back there since he was eighteen, over nine years ago. The colliers let him pass and went back to their stories, too lame or too tired to chase the possibility of a real memory down the road. He approached the High Street with the hold-all strap in one hand and Terence's fingers trapped in the other. They passed small clusters of men standing outside empty shops, looking disorientated, bleached. They were in a state of shock, as if an earthquake had levelled their town, left them homeless. The old glassworks' windows were broken, the Vaudeville Theatre and cinema boarded-over and up for sale. Every second shop was permanently closed. These were the shops he stole sweets from, bought groceries for his mother, cigarettes. The small businesses of Mrs Parry, Mr Beynon, the Italians who used to lend his father their Caruso records. He lost count of the houses with estate agent signs outside, themselves getting battered. The chapel and the police station were shuttered too. It was a dead town, a third-world pocket of Britain, not unlike certain areas of Belfast.

The house on Craig Street where Evan was raised stood above the road on the hillside, squatting in the centre of a terrace of two-up, two-down houses with outside toilets and no bathrooms. Evan counted eighteen in the row of twenty houses – gutted, abandoned, boarded-up. He led Terence, who had walked from the bus to Craig Street silently focused on the pavement, up the steps to the front door of number 17. The door was still open to the street. There had never been a key, the house never locked.

Inside the hall another door opened into a sitting room, where a coal fire in the hearth filled the room with smoke. Apart from a few more holes in the hearth rug where hot coals had fallen out of the grate, the room had not changed. The wallpaper had gone brown, to match the ceiling. Evan remembered when his father last tried to paint the ceiling, standing on a step ladder, dripping paint into his mouth. He gave up before he had finished, and never decorated again. The only cheerful character in the room was the fire, which Evan had grown up with, like a brother or a sister. It was the one source of heat in the whole house. Evan went to stand next to the fire and warmed his back.

Terence sat on the threadbare sofa swinging his legs and staring into the fire. His little corduroys were grass-stained at the knees and his white socks had turned an ash-grey. Evan had not brought a change of clothes for either of them. You could live in fatigues for weeks. But mufti was not so durable, nor camouflaged.

It was odd to see his son there, a new generation on the old motley sofa where Evan had grown sixty inches, looking into the same sulphurous flame, drawing up plans for his future. Even at Terence's age he was continually projecting himself somewhere else, into someone else's shoes, like a stunt pilot's or a boxer's, trying to work out how he could take Cassius Clay through fifteen rounds. He wondered about the content of his son's thoughts. Did he have a blueprint of his future gummed behind his forehead? He looked as if in conference with himself. Evan came straight out and asked him. 'What are you thinking about, Terence?'

'Mummy's going to be angry with me when I get home.'

Children today all live in the present continuous, Evan thought heavily. 'You'll be meeting your grandfather soon. Never mind about your mother.'

On the mantelpiece stood a framed photograph, the single reference in the room to Evan's existence. The picture had been snapped from the ground during a NATO parachute exercise over Norway. Evan's parachute canopy was just developing, the Hercules pulling away above at four hundred feet, the sky around him crystallising with countless blossoming parachutes. Evan remembered the day well, how he had to take the last parachute in the hanger, being the last in the queue. The parachute had fallen off the duck boards and lay in a pool of greasy water. Moreover, its red safety inspection tag was missing. When he told the CO that he thought his chute may be unsafe, the CO told him he was jumping anyway, with or without it. In the aircraft, Evan vomited from the Artur, pressurisation and terror. Over the dropping zone, he hooked up and broke into a flu-like sweat. The dispatcher pushing him out of the door felt like the final brush with human life. His legs were swept sideways in the slipstream and he plunged horizontally towards the ground. Then he felt the harness bite at his shoulders. He looked above him and saw the canopy opening. The photographer down below on the DZ had captured that moment, the 1/125th of a second in Evan's life when he was truly happy, when he had been totally free of fear. Behind the frame hung a St Christopher medallion on a chain. His mother had died before the photograph was taken. So it had to be his father who put it there.

As if on cue Evan's father stepped into the house from the street. He took a swipe at the room, his large shoulders crashing into the door frame and the lampstand. The old man took a moment to make a positive ID of the persons sitting in his house, then his mouth dropped open and a strand of yellow-grey hair flopped out of his oil-stained cap. He and Evan remained standing at each end of the small room for several seconds until Reynold Price raised the bottle of milk in his hand. 'Last one Mrs Rees had in the shop' he said, uttering the first words Evan had heard his father speak in ten years.

'Lucky, then.'

'What's that?'

'Lucky to get the last bottle.'

'No . . . no . . . I'm not lucky.'

'Shall I make some tea with it?' Evan offered.

'You make tea?' Reynold replied incredulously.

'I can make tea.'

'So can I. I know where everything is.' Reynold's deep and mellifluous voice sounded rather brittle now, trying to corral a wide range of conflicting emotions.

'This is Terence, by the way. Terence . . . meet your grandfather.'

The old man looked at his grandson for the first time and said, 'His hair's a bit long for a boy.'

'He's only five, dad.'

'He looks like a girl.' The old man huffed and made for the kitchen holding the bottle of sterilised milk in both hands, at arm's length.

'Can we stay for a few nights, dad?' Evan asked through the wall.

'Your room upstairs is empty.'

Evan turned the television on for Terence with the volume at a whisper. A pale football floated silently across the luminous screen. Evan wondered what match it could be, since it wasn't Saturday. Then it occurred to him that he didn't know what day it was, for sure. He didn't know what was going on in the place where he was born and raised, he didn't know what was happening in the world and he did not know what day it was. Perhaps it was best that way. Sometimes it was best to know nothing at all.

On top of the television were more framed photographs of his sisters, Dilys and Beth, with a gaggle of children whom he did not recognise. There was a picture of his mother, her great girth dressed in black, with a look of explosive frustration on her face, towering over her husband sat in a chair, resting his hands on a walking stick. Evan stepped away from the TV set, thinking how much he hated the camera.

Evan climbed the stairs to his old bedroom. The room was unheated, like the rest of the house, and felt damp. Nothing had altered there either. A narrow bed against the window was covered in the same lime-green eiderdown and the same WWII army issue brown blankets. On the wall was his poster of Tommy Farr, the Welsh boxer who went the distance with Joe

Louis, and who once said, 'Every time I think of Joe Louis, my nose begins to bleed.'

Farr was the man whom Reynold most wanted his son to emulate. In his time, Reynold had been an amateur middle-weight, often travelling hundreds of miles to fight after a twelve-hour shift underground, returning from an epic battle to go straight back down the pit without a wink of sleep, just ten rounds of nourishment between shifts. He had also been a prop for Aberech RFC, a tenor soloist with the Brecon Male Voice Choir and an NCO in the Airborne Regiment during the Second World War. A thoroughbred Welshman, the pedigree son of a pit town, bordered by steel towns. The society of men was the only society he saw fit to subscribe to. Grooming Evan to follow in his footsteps was a natural act for any father. And he succeeded to the greater extent. Evan was a champion junior welterweight, an outside-half for Aberech schoolboys and a good airborne soldier. But since the day he left home, Evan had never returned for a visit, nor telephoned, nor written. He told Celia that both his parents had passed away. He tore up all the letters his family penned to him c/o The Parachute Regiment's HQ in Aldershot.

Evan went back downstairs where his father was attempting to present a decent tea on a fold-leaf table in the living room. His hands shook the crockery more fiercely than the sea had shaken the crockery on Colin's boat. He cut some slabs of fruit cake and poured the milk into the cups from the bottle.

They sat down to tea around the fire. Evan handed Terence some cake and looked into his tea cup without drinking. The tea was a golden colour and thick as syrup. As he stared into the cup he tried to think why he had come here in the first place. There were other places he could have gone to ground. He couldn't put it into words for himself and so would have no chance explaining it to his father, if he asked. It seemed as though he'd followed a powerful instinct, which led him to his old front door in Craig Street. Perhaps he foresaw the end of something.

Terence's eyes were fixed onto the television and Reynold's onto the hot coals in the grate. His false teeth clicked as he ate.

'Still a good fire, Dad,' Evan said.

'Aye.'

'What do you think of the lad here?'

Evan's father turned his head to give the boy a sliding moment of his time. He turned back to face the heat. 'If I could see more of his face, I could tell you.'

'It's the way they wear their hair nowadays.'

'You wear it short.'

'This is a military haircut,' Evan stumbled, tried in vain to backtrack, retrieve his words. He had given his father a cue for the one subject he didn't want to enter into.

'Have you made an officer yet?'

'Only a captain.'

'A captain will do. A captain will do very nicely.'

'I don't want this cake,' Terence tuned in.

'Then leave it,' Evan said.

'I don't like the little black dots in it.'

'Currants,' said Reynold, addressing his grandson through his father.

'Just leave it,' Evan repeated.

'Can I have something else to eat?'

'There's nothing here,' Reynold said moodily.

'I'll get you something later from the shop.' Evan took the plate off his son's lap and stuffed what remained of the cake into his own mouth.

'Where was your last posting?'

'South Armagh.' Evan coated the words in crumbs.

'When did you finish the tour?' Reynold pursued.

'I haven't.'

'On leave then, are you?'

'I'm not on leave, Dad.'

Reynold rested his chin on his thumb and tapped his lip with a forefinger. He felt the temperature of the tea through the cup with the other hand, decided it had cooled and drank the whole lot in one swig. 'If it's not leave, and you haven't completed the tour, then what are you doing here?'

'Leave it be, Dad.'

'First time home in nine and a half years and you won't answer my questions? You owe me that at least.'

Evan braced himself. 'I've gone AWOL.'

Reynold grew very still. The tea cup stopped rattling in his hand. He did not take his eyes off Evan for one second. As Evan shrank, his father seemed to grow in stature, grow even younger. 'AWOL from active duty!' Reynold said after the long pause. 'In my day, that carried a mandatory death sentence by firing squad.' Reynold spoke very slowly, as if to avoid equivocation, as if he wanted his son to take heed.

'My friend Ashley Bean told a cracker of a lie,' Terence butted in from another time, another country. 'He said he asked the vicar if he could sleep on the church roof to keep an eye on our tree den we built. And he said the vicar said yes! He slept there all night. That's what Ashley said, anyway.'

'I wanted to see my boy here, Terence.'

'What rubbish is this?' Reynold's cup began to rattle again. He rose to his feet, walked past Evan and thumped his cup and saucer down on the table top before vacating the room. 'What rubbish!' he bellowed from the kitchen.

'Terence – go and play outside for a while, there's a good boy.'

'I want to watch "Play School".'

'No, go into the garden.'

'I don't like this house. There's nothing to do. I wish I'd brought my bike.'

'It was too big for you anyway.'

'I still wish I'd brought it.'

'Well you didn't.'

'Do I have to go outside still?'

'Yes please.' Evan was anticipating a show-down any minute with his father. He didn't want Terence taking any shrapnel. 'Come with me to the shed. I have something to show you, that you'll like.'

They slipped past Reynold in the kitchen out of the door and into the garden. The garden was a twenty-foot strip of overgrown grass dominated by a tool shed and lavatory. An alleyway the other side of the wall divided the terrace from the next row of houses. Beyond that rose a sheer black flank of mountain.

Under a tarpaulin wrap in the garden shed was Evan's motorcycle. He wasn't sure if it would still be there. But no one had moved it in ten years and it looked in mint condition, sitting on blocks, its deflated tyres six inches off the floor. A Honda 750 Four with a single specialised exhaust hitched up under the pillion seat. Evan checked there was fuel in the tank and oil in the sump before depressing the kick start a few times. He turned on the ignition, but as expected, the battery was dead. He heaved the machine off the wooden blocks and tried kick starting the engine. After a few minutes he gave up on that and removed the four spark plugs with a wrench. He cleaned the plugs first with a rag and then a wire brush. He unscrewed the ignition cover and cleaned the points with an emery cloth and adjusted the gap. Finally he pumped up the tyres with a foot pump. 'Keep your fingers crossed, Terence.'

'Is it a real motorbike?'

'I hope so. Hold the door open for me.' Terence could barely hold back the door of the shed as Evan wheeled the Honda out, across the patch of lawn into the lane. The lane was on a gradient and Evan ran the motorcycle down with the gear in second and the clutch in. Near the bottom he released the clutch and performed a side-saddle mount simultaneously, to weigh down the rear wheel. The wheel locked despite Evan's weight and he fell over with the bike, breaking the front left-hand indicator. He cursed loudly and lifted the bike back into an upright position. He turned the bike around and pushed it to where Terence was waiting.

He repeated the bump-start unsuccessfully three times until the engine fired on the fourth run, letting out a cloud of black smoke from the exhaust. Evan rode back to where Terence was swinging back and forth on the gate, his head tipped down, unimpressed by his father's triumph.

Evan lifted the bike onto its centre stand on an area

of concrete in the gravel drive, then mounted Terence in the saddle. He was so tiny he had to lie flat across the petrol tank to reach the handlebar throttle grip, which Evan showed him how to twist and release. Indicating the revs counter, he warned Terence not to take it over 5,000 rpm, then left him there astride a 750cc engine. 'Warm her up for me, Terence. I'm going inside for a moment.'

The old man was brooding in a deckchair on the front porch, his knees covered by a grimy tartan blanket. He seemed to be staring across the road into the valley where his colliery had been. It was a travesty, the way the colliery had been vacated, leaving behind a tangle of headgear, conveyor belts, plant machinery, corrugated tin sheets and steel pipes – all coated in a black film of coal dust. A bulldozer was patting the slag tip down, pushing it into the side of the mountain, forcing streams to cut fresh beds into new black territories. It resembled a battlefield after heavy infantry bombardment.

Evan sat on the steps at his father's slippered feet and lit a cigarette. 'It's a bloody disgrace,' Reynold muttered.

'It is,' Evan replied, assuming his father was referring to the mess in the valley.

'I was in the Second Parachute Battalion during airborne operations in North Africa,' Reynold continued. 'I was in the strike at Oudra in November 1942.'

'I know, Dad.'

'We had to sit it out in freezing desert while tank divisions shelled our positions and Messerschmitts performed low-flying machine gun attacks. All we had for cover were our camouflaged smocks.'

'Like a crab,' Evan muttered.

'No air cover, no support against armoured cars, lorry-borne infantry.'

'I've heard all these stories . . .'

'We had been dropped there days ahead of the first army . . .'

'Dad . . .'

'And none of us went AWOL!' Reynold finally made his pitch, reached the point he was making.

'Okay, so what?'

'Airborne soldiers are not just élite soldiers, boy, they are élite people. The first to arrive, the pioneers of combat.'

'You're talking about World War Two.'

'I'm talking about Two Para! That's your battalion and my old battalion. Family. More like family than some of your gutless uncles were ever family. Could you imagine trusting your life with your uncle Emrys? Can you see John Parry holding a rifle and risking his neck for you against an enemy, a company strong? Can you, boy? My loyalty to Two Para was as binding as my love for my children. You deserted Two Para. Your shame is my shame. That is what I'm saying.'

'World War Two is not like Northern Ireland. There wasn't a conflict there in your day, you don't know what it's like. You can't compare Northern Ireland with the campaigns of World War Two.'

'Goose Green.'

'What about Goose Green?'

'A lot of people said at the time that the Falklands was another Northern Ireland. Yet I felt proud when Two Para took Goose Green. A pride in your family when they do well in life. All the men in the village came up here to shake my hand.'

Reynold triggered one of Evan's own memories of the Task Force sailing victoriously into Southampton docks; how a crowd of women on the quayside and in small crafts bared their breasts to the squaddies on the ship. He wanted to tell his father this. 'Dad . . .'

'Don't Dad me! Not any more. You've shamed me too deep.' The old man suddenly coughed so violently it alarmed Evan, like a gun going off. It was a death rattle and full of the grief of old age. Evan studied Reynold, failing to recognise anything about his father that suggested a cold-blooded killer, a veteran of famous campaigns against the armies of Rommel and Von Arnim. All Evan could see was a sick old man, his self-esteem grounded by his miscreant son.

'The only reason British troops are in Ireland today, is to keep them bloodied,' Evan argued. 'Northern Ireland is a dummy run for conflicts like the Falklands.'

'It's not for you to question.'

'Well why not! I look around here and I look around places there and I see the same legacy of a colonising culture. The English should not be in Ireland. The Welsh have less excuse.'

'Is that why you deserted?' Reynold's eyes coruscated. 'Did you leave your men blind because of some naive polemical thinking?'

'You worked down the mine with Irishmen, Dad.'

'And Englishmen.' Reynold turned around in his deckchair to face Evan. For a moment he looked filled with compassion, as though he were sorry for his son and wanted to help him overcome his weakness. 'It's not for you to question why the army is in Ireland. You forfeited that right the day you enlisted.'

'I don't agree.'

'You went absent from active duty. You have disgraced yourself, your regiment and me.'

'Well fuck the regiment, and fuck you too!'

Evan stormed past his father on the porch, down the hall and into the kitchen, where he ran straight into a spectre of his mother, standing on the bare lino floor, gazing dreamily out of the window into the belly of the slag mountain, buttering huge mounds of sliced white bread. That is all Evan knew about his mother really. She had died in that kitchen, thirteen years ago, while making supper for everyone. The kitchen was so much her realm, she always looked out of context everywhere else. Now it was her shrine. Evan scraped his fingernail through the grease on the stove, gave one final parting thought to how she had serviced Reynold so thanklessly because his physical strength was her only protection against destitution – then ran out of the house up the garden and into the lane. There he found Terence where he had left him, prostrate across the petrol tank faithfully warming the engine, revving her into the 8,000s. Evan moored him on the back seat and took over the handlebars. He kicked down into first and drove straight off the centre stand. 'Hold onto my coat, old man.' Evan spun the machine around in a semi-circle and let out the last half of the clutch to take them down the end of the lane.

Evan weaved through the village in third gear, past old men in the square, the demolished primary school and the coal board manager's former house, now a safe-house for battered wives. A wind tracking up the valley hit them head-on and rustled through the unkept grass in the cemetery. He banked around the last roundabout in the village before the open road. As he brought the bike back up, Evan shivered from the shoulders, cranked open the throttle and sent the speedometer needle into the 80s. All his tension jerked straight out the back of his head. Road markings vanished under the front wheel and resurrected in his handlebar mirror, travelling like archers' arrows into the ever-reducing image of the village. He could feel Terence's fingers clutching dependently inside the pockets of his jacket, and through that touch, his vulnerability.

He slowed down immediately and pulled off the road, taking the cinder track that once led to the colliery. A part of the colliery was now a children's playground – surrounded by bent rusting steel and covered with broken glass. Evan parked the bike and took Terence for a ride on the roundabout. Terence clambered into the spiderweb and gripped the frame so tightly his knuckles went white. Evan sent it spinning, before leaping on next to Terence. A sombre Methodist church bell, clanging in the near distance, twisted a skein around them of dead men's maledictory music. Evan shuffled closer to Terence and put an arm around him. He felt gutted inside, like a piece of collapsed geometry, like the valley itself. Turning on that frictionless disc Evan was out of sync with everything. He could have been anywhere in the world, in any of its epochs.

He thumped his shoe down to stop the roundabout and reorientate himself. He rooted himself securely, with the realisation that Reynold had spent forty years of his life five hundred yards below his feet. Evan plucked Terence off the roundabout and carried him over to the swing.

'Not so high!' Terence protested as Evan shoved the swing.

Everything around them seemed in a state of curfew, disgraced by its own failure to survive. The Welsh weren't any good at winning. An influx of ambition could have saved the day, perhaps. But then the Welsh have never trusted that. Ambition was a visitor in town who broke up community, set son against father. Ambition was the kind of thing the Welsh take round the back of the pub and rough up a bit.

It took some effort to remember how it had been back then, how the chorus of the order of things sounded – the colliery sirens, clanking headgear, two regiments of miners, one clean, one black, passing in the village square at dawn and at dusk, their hobnail boots ringing in the cobblestone street; women stampeding their menfolk at closing time.

Evan noted the doors of the occupied houses shouldering the playground were closed and burglar alarms on each wall. There had never been such a problem as burglary in Evan's childhood, just fighting. Fighting in pubs, homes, in the street, and in his case – in the gym. Practically all young men fought in one or more of those categories. Men either got on well or they fought with their fists. It was not surprising that he found it difficult to talk to his father. He could never get around a table with him and thrash out their differences.

Evan began boxing when he was nine. His first contest was a warm-up bout at a dinner show in the

Top Rank, Newport. A three-round fight with Reynold in his corner. Many of Reynold's friends had been there, coal miners in dinner jackets with their wives in pink and white lace, eating dinner at tables around the ring. They slapped Reynold on the back and ruffled Evan's hair as they waded through the tables to make the entrance into the ring. Evan's opponent had an eight-pound advantage and a longer reach. He looked like a man to Evan. From the first bell, the other boy began to employ his advantages, building up points, pinning Evan to the ropes in a flurry of jabs. With a mysterious dull thunder in his head, Evan searched for his father behind his guard. He wanted him to take the pain away, take him home. Punters in the hall were on their feet. Evan remembered the odd sight of women's fists sprouting out of frilly evening dress cuffs, their soprano voices screaming, 'Kill him! Kill the bastard!' The one voice Evan heard clearest was his father's whisper, burrowing beneath the screams and shouts in the hall, to buzz in his ears like a secret. 'Keep in there, son. Look busy. You're doing okay. Just look busy. Back out of there now and take a walk. Jab and take a walk. One . . . two and take another walk. One . . . two, take a walk.' Evan followed the directive up to a point when a gloved fist began to wave at him, then crashed into his eyes. Evan came to sitting, his legs collapsed under him, gloves folded in his lap and urinating in his shorts. The ring became a cage and people's shouts turned into laughter as Evan's urine trickled to the edge of the canvas. The referee raised his opponent's glove and the boy's father came in through the ropes to embrace him. Which was the real trophy of the night, win or lose.

In the dressing room, Evan's father slapped him in the face and made his nose bleed. 'You shamed me, boy, in front of everyone.' Evan cried because his father had hit him. Reynold could not maintain this harshness however and tried to make amends. 'Look boy,' he said, 'if you ever get any problems, I want you to tell me about them. If you got venereal disease – gonorrhoea – you tell your father, like.'

Ten years later Evan was boxing again with a fellow recruit in a one-round all-out contest, like a bar brawl with gloves, which the army called milling. He fought a tight contest, jabbing and walking, wearing his partner down without taking a single punch himself.

Two weeks after that he jumped out of an aircraft for the first time, steadying his nerves going down before the canopy opened, whispering to himself: 'Look busy. You're doing fine. Just look busy.'

'I WANT TO GET OFF!' Terence snapped back like an elastic band. Evan had left Terence oscillating on the swing to wander away a few yards, dazed and flocked around by memory.

'Swing on, old man. I'm not going anywhere.'

'I want to get off!'

Terence began to cry. 'Ah, no . . . don't cry.' Evan ran to get him off. 'There, there.' It depressed him to realise Terence did not trust him to come back. His wife once explained the reason for this. If he doesn't trust you, she said, it's because you're the mystery in jungle-green who appears every two months for forty-eight hours, and about whom I have to say, This is your daddy, dear. How many fathers have to be constantly reintroduced to their sons?

Terence lay in the bed Evan once occupied in the small room overlooking the colliery. He tucked in the sheets around the boy and smelled dampness in the air again. It was evocative of so many mornings when he had dressed into his school uniform under the sheets.

Evan checked himself. No more reminiscing. He patted the boy's head and considered how Reynold had still not spoken to his grandson, punishing the boy for his father's sins. Evan felt a passionate fury, but let it go, let it fly.

'Why is it firemen who pull boys' heads out of railings?' Terence wanted to know.

'Firemen have the cutting gear.'

'It must be really horrible having your head pulled out of a railing.'

'They don't pull your head out, old man, they cut it out.'

'They cut your head out?'

'No, the railings. They cut the railings around your head.'

Terence shifted around in the bed, searching for a warm zone, which Evan knew from experience didn't exist. The bed probably hadn't been aired in ten years. He sat on the bed staring out of the window, waiting for Terence to drop off. He could just make out the mountain of clinker and ash in the starlight: slick black escarpments with sheep scuttling across. A coal train from the nearby phurnacite works laboured up the single track, slowing to take the bend near the stream. As it was passing beneath a derelict coal gantry, around two dozen men leapt out of bushes onto the wagons. In the moonlight Evan could just see them kicking the levers and dropping the side gates, in one synchronised movement. Tons of coal, smokeless nuggets *en route* for domestic use in England, poured out onto the tracks. Evan pressed his hands to the window with heightened curiosity and misted the glass with his breath. As the train went out of sight, the men bagged the coal and hauled it up the steep hillsides to waiting mini-vans and old Bedfords parked on the village road. Within a few more minutes they had all driven away, absorbed into the petrified landscape.

Evan was very excited by what he had seen. It was a well executed covert operation. He descended the stairs in this elevated mood and joined his father sitting in the living room, hunched over the perennial coal fire. 'I've just been watching some men ambush the coal train,' Evan explained.

'The trouble with removing the coal industry from here is, the industry was the sole reason for the communities existing.' He coughed for a long time, raking the ashes from the fire with a poker, before he could continue. 'Italians, French, Irish, Scots, English . . . we were one family. Coal was not only our livelihood, coal was our culture.'

Reynold had to pause again to empty his lungs. As he spat into the fire, Evan wondered where the old man was leading to, with this oral history. And for his sins he was given the answer. 'For generations we have raised young men for pit work, for hard physical work in the most abject conditions. It was hardly surprising that miners made good soldiers. World War One, World War Two and of course the Spanish Civil War. One hundred and sixteen Welsh miners fought in the International Brigade. Thirty-two were from this valley. Miners always distinguish themselves in battle. War heroes in these parts are two a penny. When you took Goose Green, you were simply following in that tradition.'

'Stop this, dad. I don't want to hear any more. I know where it's going to end and I don't want to hear it.'

But Reynold was on a roll now and didn't hear

Evan's plea. 'I never understood why you've never come home. I wanted you to drink with me down the club. I've stopped going there now because the young men ridicule me. Then yesterday you turn up with the boy, as a deserter from the army.' The old man back-handed a cup off the arm of his chair into the hearth, where it smashed against the flagstone. He pulled himself out of the chair and left Evan alone in the room. The old man seemed ashamed of his age, that it prevented him giving full vent to his anger. Evan listened to him climb the stairs, heaving and coughing.

Evan tilted his head back into an air still ringing with rebukes. He wanted to drink himself into general anaesthesia, but there was no alcohol in the house. Reynold never drank at home. Evan had learnt to do that in the army. He might have settled for a smoke, except he had none of them either. And so he contented himself with breathing the contentious air, conjuring visions of his father taking his bath in a zinc tub in front of the fire, while his mother scrubbed his back with a brush until the skin glowed like candle wax. Reynold's bath time was also story time, when he would relay mining incidents to Evan in a sombre tone, his face still black with coal dust, about pit ponies 'committing suicide' jumping out of cages and about the epic disasters, which would surface as history many months after the event.

Now his father was over seventy years of age. An old warrior, drunk on history, cocooned in a dying community.

At 0600 hours Evan crept up the stairs to his father's room. The floorboards creaked in the bedroom and his father stirred in his sleep. Evan was concerned about waking the child in the other room. Without taking any clothes off he got into his mother's old bed and pulled the blankets over his face. He fell asleep as dawn began to suck out the darkness.

Reynold was not there when Evan opened his eyes. His bed had been smartly made and the curtains drawn to let in the light. He reached down to the floor for his watch and discovered it was noon. Six hours of crapulous sleep. He lay in bed without moving, savouring the feeling of well-being, the feel of his body under the skin. For the first time in years he didn't feel a stranger in his own flesh.

Evan got out of bed after a few more minutes and went to find Terence. He was not in bed either, which was natural. Evan went through his old drawers and found an Aran sweater to put on. Pulling the sweater over his head he chanced to see out of the window a Land-rover parked in the street. A camouflaged Land-rover. He sucked in air and backed away from the window, as if the light itself was a snake in the grass. Evan removed his jacket from the hook on the back of the door and eased his arms into the sleeves. He put his hand into the hold-all to retrieve his pistol and something clamped onto his finger, sending shock waves of pain into his head. He gasped and fell backwards onto the floor, with Terence's crab, George, hanging onto his index finger by its claw. 'Fucking hell! Jesus . . .' Evan flicked his wrist hard and sent the crab flying. It hit the wall and slid down to remain motionless at the foot of the bed. With renewed urgency he gathered himself, holding the mouth of the bag wide open, so he could see his pistol first before lifting it out by the barrel, pinching it between his fingers just as the crab had clamped onto him. He stuffed the Browning in his belt, and the penknife belonging to Colin he dropped into his pocket.

He struggled furiously against his instinct to bolt. Instincts could let you down in moments like these. He had to project himself imaginatively into the near future. The motorbike was parked in the lane at the back of the house; the Land-rover was in the front. He couldn't see the provost, Terence or his father, so calculated they were all together, probably in the living room. That was good, he could work around that. He had to split them up.

He returned to his father's bedroom, the floorboards protesting under his feet. He stopped by the window, listened, heard silence, then opened the sash window. It squeaked and rattled as the window came up. Evan climbed out and jumped onto the lawn below. It was a fair old height, and so Evan took the sting out of the landing by rolling over, swinging his legs over his head. In one move he was up again on his feet, running in a zigzag, drawing the fire of voices that wavered behind his head. He ducked into the lane where the Honda was parked with the key in the ignition. He managed to turn the key, roll the bike off the centre stand, kick start her and get into first gear before a violent punch was landed to his kidneys. The space immediately in front of his eyes went black and his hand slipped off the clutch. He slumped across the tank as the bike lurched forward. He hit the wall, glancing off the brickwork, tearing his trouser leg against the pebble dash. The impact brought him back to the surface, in touch with a threatening situation. He opened the throttle and immediately had a fight on his hands to right the bike, get it on a straight course as the wall on the other side of the lane came closer. He pulled that off, using his right foot to kick away from the wall. He could see the mouth of the lane now and opened the throttle wide. The front wheel lifted two feet off the ground. Evan reached the end of the lane and braked. As he was turning the corner he looked behind to see two uniformed MPs running after him, about ten metres away. Then they braked hard and came about, running back in the direction of

99

the garden gate. Evan now knew he could get to the front of the house marginally quicker than they could run to the back. Evan raced around the terrace and came alongside the Land-rover, which smelled hot. He flicked out the side stand and leaned the bike onto it. At the top of six stone steps, Evan found his father in the porch with a locked jaw, and just behind him in the house, Terence. 'Out the way, Dad,' Evan said with effort.

'You can't take this boy where you're going!'

'You haven't said a word to him since we arrived. What do you care?' Evan countered, echoing Celia's renunciation of himself. It took Evan just one second to make that connection, by which time he had pushed past the old man and grabbed the boy in his arms. As they were retreating down the steps to the street, Terence suddenly asked, 'Why does a willow tree weep, Daddy?'

'What!'

'Because it wants to be a poplar tree.'

Terence's joke cost Evan a valuable second. He put Terence up front on the saddle and ensconced the boy between his arms and thighs. He found a gear and pulled away as the provost took the steps in one bound.

After several miles of rational, fast driving the road was blocked at a level crossing. Evan cruised along the queue of waiting cars and pressed his front forks against the barrier. There was no sign of the RMP. He relaxed a fraction, playing the gear stick until he found neutral, let out the clutch and stretched his hands behind his head. As he cracked the bones in his fingers, he heard Terence say, 'I'm cold.'

'We'll stop soon.' Evan turned around in the saddle to check the rear and saw the Land-rover pitching towards them on the wrong side of the road. He allowed himself time to smile, then put his hand back to the throttle, squeezed in the clutch, engaged the gear box, watched the green light vanish on the dash and cut around the barriers, beating the train across the rails by a heart beat.

On the other side he let out a scream. He was losing footrest rubber on the bend in the road and breaking the speed limit before he'd even kicked out of first gear. As he was overtaking a line of trucks a mile on, dead leaves flew up from their rear wheels and stuck to his face, blinding him for a second. He was clocking 90 mph, on the wrong side of the road, approaching a sharp bend. A car appeared head-on, shaving them so close Evan could have licked the driver's ear. He pulled the bike down, through half an inch, and the car's rear wing brushed his thigh, like a bull dodged by its matador.

The road was clear ahead in front of the truck. Evan opened the throttle until it stuck and then opened it a millimetre more. Insects, drops of rain stuck into his face like needles. On each side of the road the line of trees disappeared suddenly and ploughed fields met the eye. In the distance the Brecon Beacons welded with a grey sky and the road vanished into a pinhead. The only object moving in this landscape was Evan at 115 mph, with Terence riding shotgun, shouting for all his life: 'Don't go so fast. I said don't go so fast!'

SEVEN

In a one-street village in the Brecons, Evan posted a letter – penned in a twenty-four-hour fever – to his father, of contemporary significance but ten years late. To Colin Priddey he sent a telegram with exact coordinates of where he'd gone to ground – read off an Ordnance Survey map pinned to a Welsh Tourist Office board. He wrote no message; his father's letter had exhausted him. He left Colin to decide what to do with the coordinates, if anything at all. Evan felt better just for letting him know where he was. It felt less lonely knowing someone in the world you could trust had a link if they needed it. As he was leaving the post office, he caught a reflection of his face in the steel-framed magazine shelf. He was quite alarmed by it. His face was smeared with oil and mud

– like cam-cream, his lips were cracked and a week's growth on his face threatened to catch up with his crew-cut. He got out of the shop quickly and followed a woman along the pavement, her bag brimming with fresh vegetables. He stuck on her heels until she disappeared into one of the terraced houses. A family of ceramic ducks was nailed to a pea-green wall inside the hallway. Children's laughter, a patriarch's forbidding note from within touched him deeply.

He returned across the Brecon Beacons through the MoD training areas on Mydd Bwlch-y-Groes Road. DO NOT STOP OR GET OUT OF YOUR CAR signs were posted at the side of the road. He drove slowly, savouring the landscape as mountain ranges blushed under the shadow of fast-moving cloud. The morning sun zeroed in on a Marine's steel canteen and exposed the positions of his section down on the river below the road. A tank and several armoured personnel carriers left the artillery ranges for the main road. Evan drove to where the ranges ended, turned down, crossed a small stream and stalled the Honda outside a derelict farmhouse on the civilian side of the MoD perimeter. The air was very still and quiet. The stream sparkled as it cut through banks of dead-nettle, foxgloves and purple thrift. Hawthorn trees were blooming around the building.

Dwarfed by hills, the redoubt was made with thick stone walls, small windows – now covered with corrugated tin – and a slate roof. An OUT OF BOUNDS notice, framed in red, was nailed to the wall. Evan curled back an edge of corrugated tin over the door-way and climbed in. The large timber he had left on the fire was burning. In the firelight, Terence was sitting up on a mattress of ferns, his coat buttoned up under the neck, pink from sleep, hair tousled and rubbing his eyes. At his feet was the pistol, which had worked itself out from under the ferns. Evan swept down on it and concealed the weapon in his trouser pocket.

'Are you still a soldier?'

'Not at the moment.'

'Then why have you got a gun? Soldiers have got guns.'

'Military instincts, Terence. A little harder to shed than a uniform. Come outside with me and I'll show you how to use it.'

'I'm hungry.'

'So let's go and shoot breakfast.'

'You said you'd buy me a cake from the shop.'

'Well, yes. But the shop was closed, old man,' Evan lied. He had forgotten all about the cake, was a bad victualler.

Evan trotted Terence up the hillside behind the farmhouse. The terrain there was monotonous dead ground, every fissure waterlogged, holly bushes and hawthorns the only vegetation – gnarled into black skeletal shapes. Evan was uplifted by this landscape, the scene of his own para-training years before. Such a place could strip a man of his resources very quickly. The terrain was a test of character. A place with no forests, caves, variable features – no disguises at all. An uninhabitable ghetto dulled by the same wind that chapped the lips of Roman legionaries. Up there you could find out what kind of animal you were. Evan knew no place like it. Moreover, he felt an odd security being in the military's own back yard, less conspicuous somehow. Squaddies in the Brecons were too preoccupied with dramatic training adventures, battle marches, night patrols to be bothered about a man and a boy roughing it in a derelict. That was how he would have felt, anyway, and it helped him relax, that no one really cared who they were.

Evan spotted grey fur under a holly bush. He put a brake on Terence, took out the Browning, thumbed off the safety and squeezed off a single round. His hand tickled from the recoil and the rabbit toppled over. Out of the surrounding bushes a motley collection of birds retreated in alarmed flight. A thin trace of smoke curled in the air from the pistol. Evan inhaled the cordite. It was a good kill. He had shot the rabbit from sixty metres with a 9mm. At that distance it was lucky he hit anything at all. In the bush the rabbit lay on its side, eyes wide open and staring at a point deep inside a warren hole. A tiny patch of blood glistened at the side of its neck. Evan picked up the rabbit by the ears and carried it down the hill.

Behind the farmhouse, Evan drilled his penknife into the rabbit's throat and pulled the blade through its belly. The intestines fell out stinking. He peeled off the hide, inside out and over the feet. He held up the cleaned meat for Terence's approval and saw that the boy was about to fade out on him. 'What's wrong?' Evan snatched his shoulder.

'It makes me feel sick!'

'What does?'

'That . . .'

'What, the rabbit?'

'It makes me feel sick.'

'Don't be silly.'

'It's disgusting!'

'If you're going to eat meat, you might as well learn how to kill it too.'

'I don't want to eat any of it.'

'Terence, it's all we've got to eat. You have to eat it. It'll look better when it's cooked. It will look like chicken.'

The red flags went up over the ranges as they climbed into the farmhouse. There was to be some music with their breakfast.

Evan lay the rabbit on a makeshift barbed wire grill over hot ashes and turned it periodically with a stick.

Fat dripped off the meat onto the ash, which ignited, casting a warning light on Terence's harried face. Evan hoped a full belly would improve his desultory air.

He carved off the first layer of flesh as soon as it looked cooked and offered some to Terence. But Terence refused. 'You've got to eat something.'

'I don't want to eat that.'

'There is nothing else.'

'I don't want it.'

'Then starve! I'm eating it. Look . . . I'll show you.' Evan snatched the rabbit off the grill and sunk his teeth into the flesh. He didn't care if it was cooked or not, he was so furious. He ate wildly, spreading grease and charcoal around his face, then tossed the carcass onto the fire. 'All gone. Too late to change your mind now.'

Terence crawled onto the ferns and lay down, sucking his thumb voraciously. 'I want to go home. I don't like it here,' he managed.

'We can't go home.'

'I want to see Mummy.'

'Why do you want to see Mummy all the time? Aren't I your parent as well? Aren't I an important person to you? I can do what Mummy does.'

'Mummy doesn't make me kill rabbits. Mummy's a kind person. You make me eat horrible things and you don't have any toys. I want to go home. I want to go home. I hate it here, I want to go home! I don't like this house, it's too dark. It's got ghosts and it's dirty.' Terence burst into tears and threw himself face down into the ferns.

'There are no ghosts here, Terence . . .'

Terence turned his back against Evan to face a darkened wall, so much more preferable to his father's countenance, and his body convulsed with sobs. Just what Celia did when she was pregnant, Evan noted. The evidence was mounting against him.

After a long time Terence stopped crying and turned into stone. Evan poked him in the ribs to provoke him into showing some sign of life. Even sobbing was preferable to this corpse-like stillness. But Terence was unhinged and didn't seem to feel anything at all.

Evan lay against the wall, defeated. He now knew what the bottom of a dry well tasted like. And he could feel himself grow weaker, minute by minute. He was a deserter who felt deserted by something himself – by love, by his son, by hope: one and the same thing really. By the sound of it, half the British army were mobilising for rigorous exercises outside. He fought with a desire to go and join them, to forget himself in noise and movement. Artillery shells began exploding their targets at the rate of his pulse.

Invariably the night pressed on and the temperature in the room fell. As Evan went to the window to bend the metal sheet back across the hole, a bright flare lit up the ranges for miles beyond the farmhouse. In the near distance a column of trucks passed along the mountain road, the faces of soldiers sitting under canvas white as porcelain. The flare completed its parabolic flight before extinguishing in the hills. A second flare followed, tracing a much briefer, orange line across the sky and accompanied by small weapons fire. Evan listened to the last volley, as if it were a refrain of a much larger piece of music locked in his past.

He slept for a long time and awoke feeling great distances had been travelled. The room evolved around him in the darkness. He covered Terence's legs, which had kicked out from under his coat, and put the last piece of wood on the embers of the fire.

He took a stroll outside, where a light hand stroked his head and fingered his vertebrae. He closed his eyes to prolong the tingling sensation. The sun was coming up over the dew soaked hills and began to warm his face. He spotted a whole company of soldiers running over the top of a hill a couple of miles away. Even from that distance he could tell they were paratroopers, from their style of battle march: a half-walking, half-running step any horse would recognise as a canter. One hundred soldiers moving as a single force, muscular torsos slightly forward of toes, SLRs swinging in two-hand grips, fully packed Bergens lending them a lupine contour. They filled him with a curious lust. For there was something so élite, almost holy in the way they moved up there in the mountains, scattering carrion crows off dead sheep, running for tens of miles, out of darkness into light, while the rest of the sublunary world dozed below, unaware of what was taking shape on their roof.

Evan returned to the derelict, uplifted, until Terence brought him back down with early morning complaints. 'My tummy feels like there's someone in there.'

'What's he doing?'

'Running about. Can't I have something to eat from a shop?'

'Did you know you can live for up to a month on the food stored in your body? You must drink though. You've got to keep putting fluids into your body.'

'Can I have a drink of orange?'

'We finished that carton a long time ago. Have a drink from the stream.'

'I don't like water.'

'If you're thirsty enough, you'll drink it.'

Terence climbed out of the bed of ferns, which had spread far and thinly. He looked fit and virile. The lean and hungry look suited him, Evan fancied. Outside, they drank with cupped hands from the stream. Terence shivered from the cold and the strong sunlight lent his completely white face a transparent, spectral look.

The red flags were down on the ranges, so Evan suggested they took a jaunt, to take his mind off the hunger. He also wanted to show him where he had rehearsed as an infantry soldier, where he had learnt navigation skills, fighting patrols, section attacks. He wanted to show his son something that his father was good at.

They walked to the deserted ranges where plywood targets of armed personnel had been left in their vertical attack positions. When operational, Evan explained, these targets could be flipped up from behind a rampart by staff members manning the control hut. The targets moved along a rail, powered by a chain belt. 'When they come up, they come up at three o'clock, six o'clock or straight ahead – within a sixty-degree arc of fire.' Without checking if his son had got the drift, he continued: 'Okay, Terence, this is a fire and manoeuvre exercise. We're a two-man section moving onto enemy positions. We run a few metres, go straight to ground and squeeze off two rounds each. Two rounds . . . double-tapping. Ready? Hold your rifle across your chest . . . run!'

'Will they think I'm a German?'

'No . . . now run!'

Terence began to run beside his father, holding an imaginary rifle across his chest, as his father had instructed him. 'Now!' shouted Evan. 'Go for cover!' Evan dived to ground, skidding across the grass, and made the noise of two rounds exploding. Terence came to a stop, went down on one knee and gently lowered himself next to Evan. He was smiling a little, which pleased Evan immensely. 'Keep your head down, old man,' Evan whispered theatrically. 'Stage two. You give me covering fire as I move closer to the target. When you see me going to ground and take over the cover-fire role, I want you to get up and run like hell over me and eat dirt ten metres ahead. Got that? Okay, let's go.' Evan sprang onto his feet and began to run in zigzag formation, listening to the automatic rifle noise on Terence's lips behind him. He dived then turned to see Terence running up. 'Don't fire on the run, man!' Evan was up again before Terence had properly passed and together they bayoneted the Soviet infantryman painted on the plywood board.

Panting and happy, Evan debriefed Terence. 'A bit slow getting there old man, but it's not speed that counts so much as endurance,' he said, repeating what he himself had been told by his CSM, eight years ago, after collapsing during a metal stretcher carrying race.

'There is nothing wrong with collapsing trying to finish,' was the CSM's debrief. 'Better than finishing with something to spare, like you four sons of bitches who won it. "Never give up" is the spirit of the airborne soldier.'

A light aircraft circled overhead at a low altitude,

RUSSELL CELYN JONES

then disappeared over the hill. Terence followed his
father in a battle march, deeper into MoD territory.
Evan had to run on the spot occasionally to let Terence
keep up, overcome heights and rocks. After five minutes they reached the top of a steep escarpment of
red clay, four or five metres high. It gave Evan a bright
idea. 'Hey, Terence, how would you like to jump down
there? Like your old man from a Hercules aircraft?
You want to go airborne, old man?'

'What's airborne mean?'

'Exit, flight, landing, that's all there is to it. Imagine
you're in the belly of an aircraft, eight hundred feet
above the dropping zone. Stand up in the first stick
when ordered and clip on your strop to the steel
cable running along the side of the fuselage. Do that
now. Can you feel the monster in your stomach as
you look out of the hole in the side of the plane? Red
light comes on, then green . . . Go! Go! Go! you hear
the dispatcher shouting as the stick shuffles toward
the door. You get a mighty push in the back and into
the blue air. Keep as symmetrical as poss, old man.
Arms folded over the reserve chute and start the
safety count. One thousand, two thousand . . . you
feel a nibbling sensation at your shoulders followed
by a jerk no sharper than a fair-sized trout on the end of
a fishing line. Three thousand . . . check canopy! Hold
the harness and look through the rigging lines to see if
your canopy is developing in the air currents. A thing

114

of divine beauty, old man, inhaling the wind, with the sun shining through it. You want to try that?'

'Yeah!'

'From exit to landing, it's all over in thirty seconds at eight hundred feet. Don't forget your flight drill and keep your toes up, knees bent for the landing. Red light on . . .' Evan looked at his boy beside him, imitating Father in the game, clipping on his imaginary strop. Just as Evan had imitated his father. The connection clunked loudly and Evan saw his son in that second so clearly, so painfully, he was possibly realising him for the first time. A feeling of power overcame him, from just being with his son. This was what was possible, after all.

He laughed at the revelation, laughed by Christ! letting out a wild, condemned gob of laughter. 'Green light on . . . Go!' Evan pushed him in the back off the top of the escarpment. Terence fell away from him like a stone, his arms above his head; eyes hooked into Evan's eyes, searching for the canopy that would never open. His body swung in mid-flight . . . one thousand, two thousand . . . and hit the ground on his back, a Roman Candle. He lay still and insensate, red dust swirling around him.

Then it was Evan who was freefalling through the rigid air, his response mechanical as he touched down on earth, flexing his knees, transporting the weight of his body over the right thigh, landing on his back, legs squeezed together and passing over his head to complete the roll. He craned himself onto his legs, which had already begun climbing to where Terence lay.

Evan swooped him into his arms. He fell with Terence across his chest. Terence's mouth was wide open and silent like a fish dying out of water. The escarpment seemed to soar above their heads, reaching the height of an average two-storey cottage. There was some blood on his face. Evan seized the boy tightly in his arms. He didn't know what else to do, felt so ill-equipped. He just hung on desperately. After what seemed a very long time, a whooping noise discharged from Terence's throat. It sounded like a dog barking at first, then a cockerel. Terence held his head back, exposing his throat to Evan and screamed, his dance medal up around his neck. Evan rocked him to and fro. 'There, there,' he said. Terence flailed his arms and kicked his feet against his father in his struggle for air. After a few more moments, Terence's cries achieved a rhythm. Evan took his hand in his, screwed up together in a reef-knot of pain on the clay bank.

When Terence fell asleep Evan began to weep like a grandmother.

He felt a deep and alien sympathy for his wife. She had warned him about the army. She said it could only teach him the wrong trade, the cruel skills. The army was enemy all along.

Evan watched the sun move. Terence, awake now, spoke for the first time. 'I'm dying,' he said.

'You're not dying.'

'I want Mummy.'

Evan nursed him close-to, but Terence struggled against the heat of his father's embrace. 'I'm going to tell Mummy you threw me off that mountain.'

'Tell her I forgot to take you through the landing drill, if you have to tell her anything.'

'Was it as high as a dinosaur?'

'No, of course not.'

'I'm still going to tell Mummy.'

Evan tried to distract him by talking about tranquil things. But Terence wanted to leave the firing ranges, the Brecon Beacons, that place of peril and wind. It had become macabre. Or was it his father who terrorised him?

The clouds had darkened the night sky. The only light in the room was the lambent glow of the fire. Evan had kept it going for all the days they camped out there. He padded the boy with dry crumbling ferns and lay for a moment at his side. 'Ashley Bean and Deanne Webb are in love,' Terence surprised him.

'Who are?'

'Don't you remember? I said I saw them in Bell Meadow with his arm around her. I felt a little bit

117

sick when I saw it. I thought Ashley Bean wouldn't come round to our house again.'

'I'm sure he will.'

'I wish Ashley was here. I still don't like this place.'

'It's the last place on earth God created.'

'Is it really?'

'Well, it ain't Bethlehem, old man.'

'Will you tell me a story?'

Evan lay down and told Terence the story of the gypsy who was asked to make four big nails. After he had finished the work he took the nails to his customer. He had handed over three before being told they were to be used for securing Christ to his cross. The gypsy ran off with the fourth nail. The gentiles mounted a search and have been looking for him ever since. It was this search that led to the persecution of the gypsy.

Terence's breathing became more phased, sonorous. He fell asleep in the middle of the story. Evan went to the window to stare out beyond the tin sheet. The sky was again lit by flares, an orange glow across the mountain ranges, accompanied by very distant artillery salvoes.

He returned to the bed and took out his pistol. He slammed the clip – kept separate – back into the handle. Then he pushed the muzzle into his ear. A whole clip of love through his head, with

Terence's finger on the trigger, was the cure he needed.

Outside the farmhouse he discharged the remaining rounds into the air. When it was empty, he once again ejected the clip and tossed the pistol into the air, as far as he could throw, into MoD territory.

One hundred metres away, close to the MoD perimeter, stood an isolated figure. It could have been a chimera, a trick of the phosphorus light of flares crossing the skyline. Evan studied the presence, which never moved, but seemed to be looking at him. His heart thumped against his ribs as he deduced it was male and probably civilian. He shouted into the night. 'Who goes there?'

'Paramedic. Know anyone who needs one?'

'Yes,' said Evan recognising the voice. 'I do.'

EIGHT

The corrugated iron sheets covering the four windows and door had been wrenched back with great conviction, to allow the morning light access to the space inside, where the fire hissed in the stone hearth and they sat surrounded by opulence: sleeping bags, blood-red ambulance blankets, pots and pans, calor gas ring, cardboard boxes swollen with food. Terence unloaded the boxes carefully, handling each item like a sacrament, naming everything, and by doing so confirmed their reality. 'Yoghurt, two pints of milk, orange juice, eggs, apple juice, lemonade, chocolate, bread, tomatoes, water in a plastic bottle, tuna fish, tomato ketchup, potatoes, carrots, green peppers, cooking oil, cauliflower, apples, grapes, two pineapples, bananas, wine, cheese . . .' Evan opened polystyrene cups of olives, coleslaw, taramasalata, pickled herrings. Terence was chanting 'Fruit cake, biscuits, peanuts, peanut butter, marmalade, a joint of meat, sausages, mushrooms, bacon, and . . . and . . .'

'Ground Turkish coffee,' Colin completed the checklist. He spread one of the blankets over the floor and selected food to be immediately consumed. Potatoes, eggs, sausages, bacon, mushrooms, green peppers. Like a scientist, he turned on the gas bottle and lit the ring. He sliced all the vegetables very thinly and tossed them into a large frying pan heating with some oil over the gas flame. Evan observed the whole thing in silence. Terence guzzled down lemonade and feasted on grapes, Edam cheese, his arm wandering over the range of food on offer. Evan watched him, ashamed he had not organised this himself.

Sitting on his heels, Colin made a fried potato pie with mushrooms and peppers. Another pan he filled with thick rashers of bacon and sausages speckled with herbs. He cracked open six eggs without breaking a single yolk. He found a place for this pan on the log fire, which immediately began to heat and filled the room with corpulent smells.

As Colin was filling a large steel coffee pot with Evian water, Evan noticed his friend's dress. His Levis were a clean washed-blue, his white shirt ironed, hair combed, chin shaven. In comparison, Terence's trousers were now a rust brown colour and torn at the knee. His blond hair had crusted like an open jar of mustard. His socks had ridden down to his ankles, exposing a rim of dirt on his legs that continued up under his trousers. Evan wasn't wearing any socks at all and the sole of his shoe had been torn off in that freefall.

Finally the three filled themselves with pork and eggs and hash potato. The water boiled in the pot and Colin poured in the ground coffee, returning the pot to a corner of the fire. The coffee bubbled and spilled down the side, black and treacly. Evan badly wanted a cup of that. He wanted a mug of strong coffee with full-cream milk and sugar. He could not wait for Colin to serve and poured out two chipped mugs, smelled the strength in the steam, topped each one with milk . . . there was no sugar . . . handed Colin his, and raised his own mug to his mouth. His hand was trembling. The coffee was so potent and the perfect temperature. He took two huge mouthfuls that dissolved in his mouth before he felt a flush like a shot in the back of the head. Seconds later the shock mellowed into a wholesome character radiating right through his skin. He was about to pour himself another mug, then stalled, looked around at Colin. 'Finish the lot. We can brew some more.' Evan took up his offer, filling his mug to the brim. He supped an inch off the top and stirred in some more milk which turned the coffee the colour of a female mallard. He

123

tore at the bread, split the wad open to fill with soft salted butter and marmalade. He sank his teeth into the bread, softening the dough with a mouthful of coffee. Only then did he enjoy what he was eating. The eggs, bacon, sausages, potato had gone down too quickly; he had been too hungry to sense it. The bread and marmalade had a simple but big taste.

He surfaced for the first time in minutes and looked around for Terence. There he was, the beauty, wiping his plate clean of egg yolk with a chunk of bread in his fist, his free hand up-ending the apple juice, which gushed out of the carton down the sides of his face and splashed onto his chest. He wiped his mouth with the back of his sleeve and quipped: 'Hands up if that was the best dinner you've ever tasted . . .'

Evan and Colin held up their hands self-consciously, imitating Terence. 'How were the sausages?' Colin asked.

'No, I'm not going to say they were marvellous. They were more than marvellous. They were wonderfully marvellous.'

Colin's face cracked open with laughter, while Evan remained saturnine. He had never made his son so eloquent. Why couldn't he inspire Terence to make such jocund remarks? 'Have more,' Colin gestured to them both. 'Eat. Eat!'

'I'm going to have some taramasalata and some orange juice to drink next. Then I'm going to eat all that cheese up with the rest of my bread. Can I have some chocolate too?'

'Anything,' Colin laughed. 'All of it.'

'Chocolate and then I'll have a piece of cake, I think. Maybe that pineapple . . . no, I'll have a yoghurt, then some pineapple.'

'Eat! Eat!' Colin repeated, before brewing another two-pint pot of coffee that if anything was better than the first. As he was pouring it out, he said, 'I've brought something else for you,' and produced an ounce of Virginia tobacco from his leather coat, and some papers.

Evan lowered his face, heavy with emotion. He took the tobacco off Colin without looking at his face and began to roll himself a fat cigarette. The paper was swollen with tobacco as he put it into his mouth and lit the end off a burning log. He followed the caffeine with a rich wad of smoke and felt himself burgeon with hope. 'Hell! Who said the body don't need drugs.' He picked up his head and laughed. 'Put another log on the fire, Terence. Let's kill that chill in the air.'

When they were all full, Colin took Terence to his car to pick up even more supplies. A few minutes after they left Evan heard a piercing laugh outside. Tentatively he approached the gaping doorway, not wanting to spook the boy's pleasure, while determined to find out the cause of it. What he saw was a miracle: Terence was cycling down the farmhouse track on that big new bicycle without help from anybody. 'Look at me! Look at me!' he chanted.

Colin was having a piss against the side of the farmhouse. 'How did he do that?' Evan asked, with hands on hips. 'It was too big for him last week.'

'What do you mean? I put stabilisers on the back wheel.'

'Stabilisers?'

'Those little wheels.'

'Ah! Now I see . . .' But Evan could not see where Colin received his childcraft from. He had no children of his own. 'Looks like you've lowered the saddle a bit too.'

'I have.'

After Terence wore himself out on the bike they returned indoors with more bags. Colin emptied a pile of new clothes out on the floor. 'Size four to six years for Terence. They should fit, shouldn't they? Four pairs of socks, trousers, pants, a couple of tops . . .' He caught sight of Evan's troubled air. 'I've over-supplied because I didn't know what you were going to do. Your telegram was a bit cryptic.'

Terence stepped out of his ruined corduroys and dirty sweater and got into new underwear and a green tracksuit. Evan helped him on with the socks. It felt good to do that little bit for him. He plucked the elastic waistband and let it slap against the boy's stomach. Colin helped Terence to break open another bag, which contained a wallet of felt pens, pads of plain paper, crayons and three picture books: *Willie the Wimp, Willie the Champ* and *Captain Pugwash*. 'I used to watch Captain Pugwash on television as a kid,' Evan told Terence.

'Did you watch Captain Pugwash on television when you were small as well?' Terence asked Colin.

'Yes I did,' said Colin.

Terence broke open the felt pens and immediately got down to drawing out his experiences. Evan asked in a hoarse whisper: 'Where did you learn to cook, Colin?'

'It's no big thing, Evan. You just decide one day to cook and start from there. Every packet of pasta has a recipe written on the side.'

'You on leave now?'

'I've got two days off. How long do you intend staying here?'

'I'm glad you reinforced us when you did. Terence was down to his last few rounds, old man.'

'You've got to take care of these little people.'

'I'm aware of that,' Evan fenced angrily. 'Where did you learn about children . . . in a book?'

'The same place where I learnt to cook.'

'And where is that?'

'In the ambulance service.'

'Oh yeah?'

'A lot of casualties tend to be very young.'

'They're sick and injured. Terence is not sick.'

'They need caring for, Evan, that's the fucking point. And you can't be an asshole when you're caring for children. The ambulance service gets hold of assholes like I used to be and turns them around in eight weeks.'

'What about cooking?'

'We cook for each other in the mess ... during shifts.'

'Sounds like a good job then, doesn't it.'

'Perhaps you should take Terence back to his mother.'

'Whose side are you on?'

Colin raised his eyebrows and took a sideways glance at Terence, sprawled out on the floor, etching a dramatic self-portrait. 'I know what I'm going to draw in the background,' he announced. 'A dark, dark forest. He's all alone in the forest.' A scribbling of felt pens filled the room as gunfire perforated the background.

'Sorry,' Evan apologised to Colin.

'Does that mean you'll take him back?'

'I won a prize for my drawing at school,' Terence interrupted.

'What did you win?' asked Colin, observing Terence's drawing of a figure surrounded by dead trees in a scorched earth.

'Five pounds to spend and an Easter egg.'

'Who gave you the prize?'

'These women dressed as chickens.'

Colin drew Evan aside. 'I wouldn't like to see you get caught here. It would ruin the boy's eyesight to see his dad tumbled into the back of a jeep. What did you bring him here for?'

'It's where we did our fieldcraft. It's second home to me.'

'Doesn't your father live nearby?'

'My father tried to turn me in.'

Colin looked perplexed and scratched the side of his eye. 'Have you finished that drawing yet?'

'I've nearly finished it.'

'When you're through we could go for a walk.'

Terence lowered his pen across the paper and looked seriously at the men. 'I don't want to go for a walk.'

'He thinks it's sinister around here. There's been nothing for him to do. No television, cinema, ice-skating, or ballet rink, whatever it is he does at home. I've had to invent details.'

Colin touched the scratches on Terence's face. 'How did you get wounded?'

'Daddy pushed me off a huge cliff. He was learning me to parachute.'

'So now you have a scar to talk about,' Colin suggested. 'See this scar on my hand? My friend Billy Cole did that with an arrow when I was six. When you get older you can tell children the story

129

of your scar. A scar is as good as a photograph for jogging memories.'

'I've been in the war.'

'If you come with us on a walk, you can take your bike. What about that?'

'All right.'

They climbed the hill at the back of the farmhouse for fifteen minutes, taking turns to push Terence on his bike across the craggy ground. The wind got up and pinned them down at the top. There were no trees or foliage for the wind to shake and it was as quiet as God up there, a silence spoilt every few minutes by small arms fire from distant ranges. There were soldiers too, in small patrols dotted about in the Beacons. They watched two red berets four hundred metres away escort a third from an observation post, tie him to a stretcher and lower the stretcher down a gulley by rope.

'I've just done a blue light shift with P.J. Sinclair,' Colin recalled. 'I love that man. Sinclair was in the Metropolitan Police for ten years before joining the ambulance service. He's an ex-hardman and you can just imagine him as a thug in the Met. Now he goes down on his knees to a casualty, touches him on the shoulder, reassures with that melodious Glaswegian voice of his. It's a pleasure to watch. Sinclair saved this butcher's life on Thursday and the butcher's wife came into the station the next day with a bouquet of roses for him. Sinclair was so overcome, the bouquet broke in his fists. He tried to catch them and pierced his face on the thorns,' Colin laughed. 'She also gave us fifty quid's worth of meat coupons. That's where I got our sausages and bacon.'

'We watched this film, which it was . . .' Terence began in a panic of remembrance. 'We watched . . . it was horrible. We watched this film in school about a boy who was knocked down by a car. He was covered in blood. And he had to stay in the hospital for three months . ' Terence squeezed the brakes on his bike. He could not go any further, so overcome by the celluloid image he'd seen.

'Let's get out of here now, Evan.'

'Where to? There is nowhere I can go.'

'It's doing no one any good to be here. Take him back to his mother's.'

'She's fucking me over, Colin. You don't understand. That woman knows no bounds, she's ruthless. I'm sure she told the provost to find you if they wanted to find me. She has used Terence as a weapon against me. She kills all the men she marries. Only now she's suffering like a woman whose child has been slaughtered. I bet she's singing like a lark!'

'I'm not with you, Evan. You've lost me there . . .'

'It doesn't matter,' Evan sighed. He was in a defence-less position. 'Take him back to your boat. I want to see my father once more and then I'll join you.'

NINE

Lying unopened on the porch floor behind the door
was his letter. He hoped it might have worked as a
bridge, where he and his father could meet. Picking
up the envelope, Evan carried it ceremoniously in the
palm of his hand into the living room.

His father was wedged into an armchair wearing
his cloth cap, scarf around his neck, resting his hands
on his belly, chin on chest, with his eyes peacefully
closed. Evan did not disturb him and just placed the
letter across his knee. The fire in the hearth looked
as though it were out, and Evan's first consideration
went into trying to save it. That fire had been kept
in by his mother, and later by Reynold, for the past
forty years, banked up at bedtime with a bucket of
coal, and revived in the early morning. It was a piece
of living history, and Evan blew into the heart of the
ashes, hoping to agitate a lukewarm nugget of coal.

After sustained effort, he managed to turn an edge of grey into orange, ignited a few sticks of wood and surrounded the burning wood with hand-placed lumps of coal. He felt dizzy from all the inhaling and exhaling, as though he were inflating a rubber dinghy.

He swivelled on his knees and looked at the old man slumped in the chair. 'Dad, I've got the fire going again,' Evan whispered, and then progressively louder: 'Dad . . . DAD! I know you can hear me. Why did you call the provost? I'm a good soldier, you underestimated me. I'm not so easily caught as that. When I'm ready, I'll walk in and give myself up. Dad, why don't you read the letter I've written you? I've explained everything in that.'

Evan noticed his parachute photograph was missing from the mantelpiece, and wondered if he had come back too late, wondered if this particular father-son relationship had failed itself.

He removed the letter from his father's knees and fanned the old man's face with the envelope. 'It's all in here,' Evan repeated. He looked deeper into his father's face and placed his ear next to his nose. Slowly he withdrew his face and began shaking his father by the shoulder. But he would not revive. Repeating the patient attention he showed the fire, Evan continued to shake him, and shake him, to shake back the life into him.

TEN

This all began routinely, with a surveillance operation; myself, a junior NCO and four new Toms doggo in a double hedgerow for two nights, keeping a derelict farmhouse under the lens, where a ground patrol had unearthed some circuitry on the weekend. We were stretched out on the grass, awaiting developments, maintaining radio silence, when I saw something move in the farmhouse with image-intensifying binoculars. I had 0115 hours on my watch. We moved out in box formation, anticipating a contact. One of the young bloods in my platoon opened fire in an accidental discharge. Things got a bit of a shambles from then on. The drills went to hell, sections split apart and the machine gunners lit up from the flank, their muck whanging past our ears into the windows of the derelict.

135

There was someone in there all right. A woman delivering her daughter's baby under a canvas sheet. One of our rounds killed the daughter and the infant was born dead. I don't know why they were there. Tinkers, no more, no less, neither Catholic nor Protestant.

Do you call that combat? See anything like that in Oudra?

I returned the men to the observation post to pack up the surveillance equipment. I made them pick up every piece of K-ration wrapping, cigarette butts – anything that might give away our presence. The OP had been twenty-five metres on the wrong side of the border.

They would have got morbid if they talked, so I kept them patrolling. We weren't due to be airlifted until 0600 hours, leaving us four hours to kill. After a mile I realised we were being followed. And I knew who it was, without binoculars. Whenever we stopped, she stopped, ran when we ran, maintaining the same hundred-metre distance.

The farmhouse went up in smoke, an orange flame spiralling out of the roof. Tinkers, they burn their dead. Her negative image reappeared in the phosphorescence of my binocular lens. A smouldering, steamy figure on the edge of a tree line, looking straight down the glasses, at me. I let them fall to my chest, yet she stayed there, in that colliery darkness, like an irritant in the corner of my eye.

The men were getting spooked, like foals in a corral of thorns. I gave the corporal orders to continue the patrol and meet me at the pick-up point with the RAF Wessex. Then I went off, wading through the bogs and bracken, alone. For who needs an army to confront a woman?

The going was tougher than I had thought. With every step I seemed to make less progress. Her image was fading and the crematorium fire in the farmhouse withering into a distant glow. Without the binoculars I was a blind man. I got close enough to pick out an outline of trees, and I saw her standing there. She seemed to be waiting for me. As I got even closer, I lost touch with what I intended to do. I stopped and tried to concentrate on retrieving lost initiative. But the harder I tried, the less confident I felt. Then the rain turned off suddenly like a tap. The moon came out and I could see her silhouetted against white rock.

With ten metres between us, she turned around and walked off into the woods. It looked as if I was going to lose her. It gave me an intense fear, like a great hunger. I jettisoned my rifle and equipment, keeping my side arm, and scrambled into the woods. I followed what I could see of her retreating figure, abandoning all thought of going back to my men.

There is some kind of gap I cannot account for.

I awoke from dead sleep under a concave wooden

ceiling, on a single berth against a wall, and banged
my head on a hanging kettle. The kettle was heavily
charcoaled, blackening my hand as I went to steady
it. A cast-iron stove with a tin chimney jutting through
the roof had spilled cold ash onto the floor. I was in
a wooden caravan, without knowing how I got there.
My tracks were all covered over.

It was daylight and thick snow had fallen on the
beach outside the caravan. I wandered around in
the snow for a while, collecting driftwood, feeling
very easy inside myself. When I returned laden with
wood, I looked first through a porthole in the caravan
and saw her kneeling in front of the stove, washing
herself with a sponge. She poured a little water from
the kettle on top of the stove onto the sponge and
drew it up her thighs, over her breasts and around the
back of her neck. She squeezed the sponge and water
ran down her spine. As she did this several times, she
kept gazing out of the window. But she didn't seem
to see me standing there. It was as though nothing
existed between herself and the sea.

I made a clatter piling up the driftwood before I
entered the caravan to find her covered in a blanket,
banking up the stove with wood.

Later I watched her sleep. I took off my para-smock
and rolled it into a pillow under her head. Her
mouth dropped open and I ran my fingers across
her discoloured teeth. She moaned from my touch,

then sat upright and chanted in her sleep: 'I can see my child in the fire. Owls is flying upside down o'er her head. They're closing her eyes with their wings.'

I tried imagining life without her. We had only been proximate a single day and I could hardly recall how things had been beforehand, see beyond her. I was frightened of the world suddenly, it had become unreconnoitred territory. I couldn't move my positions. I had to find out something about her unvoiced needs.

In the afternoon I woke shivering curled in a foetal ball. She was the first thing I looked for, but I was alone. In a wooden trunk at the horse end of the caravan I dug out from under white lace Victorian dresses and tiny children's clothes – a man's jeans, shirt and a jacket. I put on these clothes with my head bowed under the low ceiling. They fitted perfectly. I hid my uniform under the trunk and went out dressed like an artisan.

Fresh snow had bleached every stain, smoothing out stone and rock. Land and sky were invisibly stitched together, the horizon obscured by mist. I stood cocooned in a swirling globe of white. Seagulls nodded at the ground nearby. I saw footprints in the snow lead towards the sea.

I followed the footprints, almost playfully at first, then faster until I was slipping on shingle under the snow. I saw a deer drinking at a waterhole and froze not to frighten it away. Then I realised it was her, lying naked on the sand with her head buried in the shallows of the sea.

I had hoped to save her, but when I lifted her head out of the water, I saw she had been dead for some time. She had drowned herself in a pool of brine. Her eyes blazed on in the corpse, staring at a point located somewhere behind my head. I turned around and looked. Where a gap cleared in the mist behind me, the beach suddenly soared into mountain flank, capped with snow. Rooted near the top was a dead elm, its petrified branches infested with poppies. A man dangled half way between the summit and the sand from a rope tied to the tree. The mist returned and was all around again, ringing in my ears like percussion. I couldn't see the mountain any longer, just the climber suspended horizontally in air, digging his heels in, unable to go up or down. He jerked the rope and poppies rained down onto his head.

Her eyes shut in a dead face. And it occurred to me then that when I watched her bathe I had unwittingly been witness to her funeral preparations.

I knew what to do for her. I carried her corpse along the beach, the mist stalking me to the caravan. It was almost night and a lighthouse beam sawed through the fog, flashing intermittently into that little room of mourning.

She had laced a pair of baby's red canvas boots

around her neck and spun toy jewellery around her wrists. I hoofed burning wood out of the stove and threw everything combustible I could see onto the embers.

The fire had grown large and hot by the time I vaulted out of the caravan. I set off into the mist, as night evolved around me, the sea hissing softly. A large ball of flame sucked oxygen from the air, melting a hole in the snow and mist. The framework of the caravan bellied and collapsed into its own heat. Seagulls blinded by mist flew too close to the fire, changed course and dived for the cool of the sea

The ultimate failure is to outlive your children. A failure accompanied by the ultimate grief. As I made my distance, my thinking rounded on a new preoccupation. My son. Where was my son . . .

ELEVEN

In the fields women harvesters were cropping cab-
bages with machetes, bobbing after the tractor in the
shadow of the church steeple. An oilskinned figure
stretching her back held a pale green cabbage head
in one hand, knife in the other, and watched Colin's
Vauxhall run the gauntlet between the two fields of
women labourers.

The hub of the village was a cosy little hamlet of
cottages, a tumbling pub and a bakery with a five-foot
door. There was not a straight line in the place. Old
men rode about on antique Hercules bicycles. The air
smelled of wholesome aromas: hops, yeast, burning
elm. Colin pulled into a cul-de-sac and switched off his
engine. The horseshoe of newly built, semi-detached
houses blended in with the rest of the older village

by virtue of their yellow sandstone brick. Hawthorn and cherry trees in the quadrangle seemed ready to blow their tops any day now. A smell of freshly cut lawns was prevalent.

Evan sat in the back of the car for a few moments outside Celia's house, with Terence curled up asleep on his lap. Verdant copses of hydrangea, rhododendron and geranium gloved the lower half of the house with their notched foliage. A shiver, originating in his shoulders, shimmered down through his spine into his legs. This was his house too. He took a long hard look at it. It could be a long time before he saw it again.

The neighbour's front door opened and a man in shorts and a track suit top appeared. Evan slid down in the seat as the man walked to the end of his garden path, closed the little wooden gate behind him and began to run, jogging past the car, out of the cul-de-sac into the village. He reminded Evan of a story Celia had told him about her second husband, the one penned up in an asylum somewhere. He too had been a jogger, a clinical athlete who jotted his daily times for a ten-mile run into a notebook, who didn't ever smoke, drink, eat meat or unwholesome foods. But for all his athleticism he could not satisfy Celia, and she took a lover. The lover used to visit when her husband was jogging. For this was the one hour in the day he was dead certain not to return. She used to fuck him and then she'd clean the sheet.

One day Celia had left only enough time to dowse the sheet in a sinkful of water and put it into the drier. Her husband came in, pouring with sweat and dehydrated after his eight-mile run, and the first thing he did was to remove the tray from the tumbledrier, which was filled with vapour turned back into water, and drink it. 'That is pure distilled water, that is,' he told Celia. 'No impurities in it at all.'

Evan always reckoned he was drawn to Celia for being the converse of his mother – the angel in the kitchen, whose personality was washed out, distilled by servitude.

Evan watched his son sleep. It had become one of his new pleasures in life to do this. As with the house, it could be a long time before he saw him again. He might even miss out on his childhood completely. That would be a terrible sentence. Could a woman be that severe? The army wasn't that severe. Evan brushed his hand through the boy's hair, clean and shining again after a pit stop on Colin's boat, and wondered how he had managed to lose all his rights in the world. Terence muttered something and then went quiet again. Evan sighed. Thank God he'd had a son to kidnap. He felt a lucky man despite what penalties were soon to befall him.

Evan did not want to wake him. It would be nice to think of Terence waking up in an hour or two in his own bed, as if from a nightmare, with his mother there to welcome him.

Evan told Colin to keep the engine running. He lifted Terence out of the back seat and carried him to the front door. He rang the doorbell and felt himself go numb with fears. He dug deep inside himself for the courage to see this moment through.

The new front door was made of solid oak, replacing the frosted glass door he had punched out. As he was admiring the door, it opened a few inches, exposing a pair of bleached eyes. Then it flung wide open. Celia stood on the threshold and burst into tears. Panicked, Evan offered Terence to her draped across his forearms, the boy's button mouth agape, eyes closed. She began to shake and he realised that she thought Terence was dead. 'Don't wake him,' Evan said quickly, 'please let him sleep.'

The despair on her drawn pale face instantly chilled into mute rage. Evan managed to kiss Terence quickly before she took him into her arms and laid his head across her shoulder. Evan saw her breathe in the boy's scent for comfort, as he had learnt to do. She was in her dressing gown and slippers at four in the afternoon, looking more like a patient than a nurse. Her thick red hair had been yanked back by an intolerant hand and tied with a white shoelace. Celia looked as if for too long she had had insufficient air to breathe. Evan hadn't seen her like this. But then maybe he had. Perhaps he was realising her too, like Terence, for the first time.

She looked Evan up and down with an expression of contempt. In moments like those when one is looking for peaceable solutions, appearances could be crucial. Evan had turned out clean-shaven in a charcoal-grey suit and open necked ice-blue shirt. Inside himself however, he felt combat eroded.

She looked too chock-full of tears to speak. He stared at her, at the warm house stretching from behind her back, and could smell something unpleasant, like decaying meat. Then he realised it was her fear. She was only there, still standing in an open doorway, because she was too afraid to close it. He didn't want that power over anyone, and so turned his back on Celia and his son and walked away. As he passed a bed of narcissi and daffodils, he snapped off a flowering stem and pushed it into his button hole.

TWELVE

The house on Craig Street looked subdued in drizzling rain, below low-slung cloud. Evan studied the front of the house like a cine camera holding its frame, and saw himself make a million entrances and exits through the door, which had always been maroon, growing a little with each exit, clambering full-tilt down the hillside, the moonside, into the valley where the river and colliery and railway all squeezed through. The dry stone wall at the front of his house had been a rendezvous point for his father's friends who would talk and smoke late into the night after the pub before going in to sleep, and for his mother's friends who took it over by day. He remembered her pose – arms folded over her apron she lived in, with Mrs Beynon, Mrs Griffiths, Mrs Sullivan, festooned in singing gossip.

Above and below Craig Street were more parallel rows of terraced houses built like steps in the hillside. A fast-running stream cut over the rocks at the end of the terraces, tumbling and gargling with their flotsam.

Evan took the steps into the house. The porch was as far as he could get. People were packed in the hall, on the stairs, and had filled the living room. He thought he'd come into the wrong house until he made a positive ID of a middle-aged woman negotiating her way down the stairs, holding her dignity like her cigarette in its gilt holder above her head. Her grey hair had just come out of rollers. Evan's sister Beth, his senior by sixteen years, had seen him come in from the top of the stairs and was trying to force a wedge through the men packed in the hall. Her presence grew stronger as she closed in and Evan could feel his cheeks burning, where she used to pinch him in greeting a hundred years ago. Her hand appeared over the talking heads. Evan took hold and levered her through. She smiled and kissed him with easy familiarity, as though Evan had just been taking a walk around the block for the past ten years. 'Where've you been, boy?' she enquired.

'I'm sorry, Beth, the army . . .'

'Time you deserted isn't it?'

'Yes,' he smiled, 'you're right.'

'Aren't sisters always?'

'I don't know,' Evan bowed his head modestly.

'Of course they are. Older sisters anyway.'

Evan buttoned his suit nervously. He felt a stranger in this suit borrowed from Colin. A black suit, white button-down shirt and black tie. He had recently shaved and could feel the chill of the air on his face. Beth brushed his sleeve. 'You look very smart,' she said.

Evan distracted her by presenting a small school photograph of Terence. Terence was fully kitted in grey uniform and yellow and grey striped tie, the knot askew and as big as his smile. His cheeks were aflame and his eyes generous. Beth studied it carefully, then commented, 'A boy like this you should show off more often.'

'Yes.' Evan felt proud and returned the picture to his breast pocket.

'Yes! What do you mean, yes?' Beth laughed. She slapped Evan's face between both her hands. 'Ten years is it?'

'I'm sorry,' Evan said.

'I never doubted you'd come round again, and I knew you must have had your reasons for staying away. But don't be a stranger for the next decade. I don't think I could be so patient again. I'm not young any more. And none of us lives forever.'

Evan listened while reconnoitring her forgotten face. She had left home to become a teacher when he was three and was a bit of a stranger to him. An interesting stranger.

Evan's other sister, Dilys, appeared from the living room and gave a little whooping cry as she saw him. Dilys was five years younger than Beth with the same imposing physique under a tweed suit. They were not attractive women in any conventional sense. They were not attractive in any unconventional sense, either. Rather like World War Two bomber command, in lipstick, heavy powder and rouge.

'Would you like some tea, Evan?' Dilys asked.

'Okay.' Beth led him away by a finger, followed by Dilys.

He didn't recognise a face in the living room. Beth made introductions, but they did nothing to jog his memory. 'Vernon Davies . . . my brother, Evan. Councillor Harry Llewelyn . . .'

'How do you do.'

'Councillors Sean Doherty, Bryn Edwards, Olwen Morgan. And James Smith, Aberfan Disaster Committee, where dad and Jimmy originally met. Isn't that right, Jim? This is my brother, Evan, home from the wars.'

'Pleased to meet you.'

Evan's head craned on his shoulders. Strolling among strange bodies in his familial home induced in him a mild, dreamy giddiness, in which the walls and floor of the room were uncertain quantities.

'William Watkins,' Beth continued her roll call of

guests. 'This is my brother, Evan. John Jones, the present mayor. Peter Pringle, chief constable. Ted Williams, MP.'

What were mayors, MPs, policemen doing in his home? He conferred with Beth. 'Who are all these people? Did Reynold know them?'

'Yes.'

'For how long?'

'Some of them only recently, in the past couple of years. The others he knew all his life. John Jones . . . can't you remember him? He and dad started at the colliery together on the same day, in 1928.'

'I can't remember anyone. I don't recognise a face.'

'You haven't been around for a long time, Evan. That's probably why. Nobody recognises you either, I imagine. Forgotten chapters, love.' Her accent deepened whenever she was making an ironic point, as though she was able to step in and out of her background culture.

All the men in the room wore countenances as dark as their suits and drank stout from pint glasses. Two old men on the sofa, whom Evan tried, but failed, to account for, rattled tea cups on white linen cloths spread across their knees. Every conversation sounded conspiratorial; whispers rising and falling through several octaves. Beth and Dilys were still the only two females he had seen so far. Then the door of the kitchen was opened and Evan saw where the women had all got to: buttering hundreds of rounds of bread, slicing ham and cheese.

Nothing seemed to have changed, not even the clichés. He had taken flight years ago, in exasperation at those clichés, on an evening train out of there, head full of game plans to conceive himself immaculately in an English regiment, where he did eventually shed his accent and travel great distances both in terms of skill and geography.

He looked at his older sister from that perspective and realised why she had remained so secure. Beth hadn't gone anywhere for thirty years, except to Barry Education College. Which suggested to him that experience was inherently evil the deeper you went into it.

Beth waded into the kitchen and returned with the message, 'The tea is just standing a minute.'

The sponge man for Aberech schoolboys RFC was standing on Evan's port side. Evan remembered how he used to fly like a snipe across the field to a fallen player. He was a grey old man now, sipping his stout as though it hurt. 'That's Alex White standing next to me,' Evan whispered to Beth.

'He doesn't recollect you, though.'

'One down,' said Evan. 'Who are all the others?' he asked again.

'Councillors and miners, singers . . . some of them.'

'I didn't realise Reynold knew so many people.'

'It's not exceptional for round here. All these people worked and played hard together. What you see here is a dying community at its own wake. That's why the turn-out is so high,' Dilys explained.

'How've you been, Dilys?' Evan suddenly asked.

'I'm fine thank you. All the better for seeing my baby brother. So where've you been? I know we are separated by eleven years in age, but that doesn't mean we have to be separated in time, does it? It goes to reason we should make an effort. We are family after all. Why didn't you reply to any of our letters? You shouldn't neglect your flesh and blood. You never know when you might need us.' Dilys kissed him on the lips. Evan flushed hard. 'Look out the window,' Dilys continued. 'See those boys and girls playing in the street? They're all your nephews and nieces, who have been asking questions about their uncle Evan all their lives. They think you're a ghost.'

'Maybe I am.'

'Don't be stupid. And don't forget they're Terence's cousins,' said Beth, backing up her sister. 'Children for him to play with, grow up with.'

Evan looked again out of the bay window through the lace curtains, down into the street at the crowd of children playing there. They ranged in age from three to fourteen and were skipping, playing soccer, throwing stones down the valley.

'Fancy our Evan having a son. So tell us about your wife, then. Is she pretty, Evan?'

'We've split up,' he said simply.

'Oh, I'm sorry. Well there's a fifty per cent chance of it now, isn't there. You should have married a Welsh girl. The rate down here is forty per cent,' Beth laughed before slotting a fresh cigarette into her holder.

Beth and Dilys disappeared to complete their details leaving Evan alone with all the men in the living room. He wandered over to the mantelpiece to read the telegrams of sympathy. The first one he picked on was from the area manager of the coal board, Robert Nash. Evan remembered him coming to the house once, to ask Reynold what he knew about a rumoured industrial action among the face workers. Reynold had told him it was over pay. Nash then tried to be chummy with Reynold, saying face workers had the cushiest job in the pit, because their shifts were shortest. 'Long enough, Mr Nash,' Reynold retaliated, 'to lie in an eighteen-inch coal seam, twelve inches of which is water, the rest bad air.'

Evan read the telegram, the deep thumping of male voices around him mimicking the beat of his heart. He tossed the telegram into the fire because that was what his father would have done. He watched the white paper brown and burst into flames, then float up the chimney as a black wafer.

An arm crossed Evan's shoulders. All of Evan's muscles locked and he turned on his heels, in an offensive

stance, alarming the elderly man into a withdrawal out
of contact. 'Merlin Jones,' the man said, as though his
name was a shield. 'I was your headmaster, Evan. You
don't remember me?'

'Ah, yes . . . Sorry, sir,' Evan embarrassed himself.

Merlin Jones's shoulder drooped as he relaxed, now
Evan recognised him. 'That's all right,' he laughed. 'I
just came over when I saw you to say how sorry I am
about your father. We met many years ago, before
you were born actually, when Reynold joined the
education committee.'

Evan listened but couldn't contribute. He still felt
his headmaster had some kind of power over him. As
a schoolboy, Evan hunted with a wild pack of boys and
Merlin Jones caned him regularly. The ceiling in the
head's office was so low that when Jones raised his
cane above the naked arse of a child, the cane would
swish against the ceiling, giving a split second warning
to the victim to brace himself. Jones was known to the
boys as 'The Willow'.

'Rugby captain, decorated soldier, boxing champion, tenor and down the pits at fourteen, wasn't
he? You must have been very proud to have a father
like that.'

Evan did not answer, simply stared incredulously
until Jones retreated into the crowds and his place
by Evan's side was filled by John Parry, his mother's
brother. After sharing formal platitudes, John seemed

157

obliged to say, 'We brothers-in-law used to look down on Reynold at first, if the truth be known. The family used to think your mother had married beneath herself. But it turned out quite a match, didn't it? Your father and my sister.'

The little amount of daylight that had managed to find its way into the living room suddenly collapsed and died. Evan excused himself from John Parry and buried himself closer to the window. He thought about going upstairs to where the coffin lay, but decided he probably wouldn't be able to get past the people on the stairs. He chose to remain among strangers to whom he felt no allegiance, fumbling in his pockets with tiny balls of fluff. He watched John Parry's wife go over to him and erase some butter from his cheek with her lace handkerchief. He saw John Parry submit to it and felt a contempt for him.

He looked through the window at four of his nephews going down the hill on a go-cart made from pram wheels and a plank of wood. The boys all wore short trousers and short back and sides. The girls, admiring the boys for crashing into the wall, wore frocks and pink ribbons in their hair. The sight touched Evan deeply, for it was like a snapshot from his own childhood.

Evan recognised a pretty, modern face emerging from the kitchen. It was Unity, his niece, last seen eleven years ago or more, now metamorphosed into a woman of nineteen, blushing at Evan from across the room. Her thick woolly hair the colour of autumn fern, was braided in a long plait. She pushed through the room hurriedly to be blocked within a few feet of Evan by two burly old men, who were too deaf to hear her request to pass. She began to giggle and blush deeper, one cheek dimpling. Evan himself closed the gap. Unity presented him with a cup of tea. 'My mam told me to bring this to you,' she said. Evan took the cup and dried up. He did not know what to say to a girl who had suddenly become a woman.

After an awkward pause, he managed: 'Do you know all these people?'

'Not very well, Uncle Evan. Grandad was involved with them in one way or the other. He was well known, wasn't he. Still, I don't think there's a good reason for all this.'

'No, maybe not.'

'Funerals are a waste of time and money. People are better off going quietly to their graves.' Evan couldn't resist a smile for a teenager's indignation. 'All this mourning and paying of last respects . . .' Unity continued, 'it's fake. Corpses don't benefit from it. When I die I want to be cremated and my ashes released in a gale. No funeral.' She caught Evan grinning and took umbrage at that. 'Well, it's true! This is all in my grandad's honour and he can't feel a thing.'

159

'I hope you're right. Wouldn't it be a cruel jest, if once you're past the final post, you get eternally burdened with emotion.'

'We were up here just a month ago and Grandad sang for us.'

'He sang for you!'

'Didn't he have a beautiful voice. And at seventy-three. God, it was lovely. If I can sing like that at seventy-three, I'll go religious, I think. I can't sing at all.'

A man with a grey beard rippled through the crowds, holding his coat across his arm. He was calling out, 'The funeral car's here, the funeral car's here,' like a bell tolling.

'A face worker for you,' Unity said.

'How do you know?'

'He can't stand up straight.'

Beth and Dilys returned to the room to tell Evan and Unity that a private service for close family was beginning upstairs. 'If you don't mind,' Evan said, 'I'll stay down here.'

'That's all right.' Beth touched his arm. 'We've got to treat you gently . . . in case you run away again.' Unity kissed Evan and followed her mother out of the room and up the stairs.

After a few moments Evan heard the incantations of a minister from the room above his head. He dipped into a plate of crab paste sandwiches and felt the

air grow hot and moist. The house became respect-
fully silent as the oration upstairs gained momentum.
Evan was surrounded by a sea of darkness, of bowed
heads. He did not like the silence, deadly silence was
unnerving. It always seemed to foreshadow violence
of one kind or another.

Evan escaped from the house and stood out on
the front porch looking down into the street, where
the children were making dangerous runs on the go-
cart, overturning it on the grass verge. The road had
become car-ridden in the time he'd been there. Cars
were double-parked in both directions. Men gathered
on the pavements with hats in hand; there was an
enigmatic presence of fifty men in maroon blazers;
police constables diverted traffic away from each
end of the street and two undertakers were stamping
out cigarettes, leaning on the hearse. Hushed male
voices clotted in the street. It was orthodoxy, and
worrying. Evan could hear his own breathing, which
seemed too loud for the occasion. He looked out
across the valley in an attempt to make contact with
who he was.

He didn't see the casket come out, borne on the
shoulders of four bearers, until it nudged him on the
top step. He smiled at that, the old man managing to
give him a final kick in the head. Evan stepped aside to
allow the men to pass and manoeuvre the coffin down
the steps.

The rain, which had been falling almost impercep-
tibly all morning, transformed the valley into a grainy
sepia photograph. Dilys and Beth, flanking Evan on
the step, added their dash of Victorian monochrome
to the scene. Unity appeared and Evan allowed her to
press herself against his chest. The men in maroon
blazers grouped into a block and began to sing. It
was Reynold's old choir and a conspicuous space
in the middle of their ranks was left gaping, as the
coffin reached the street. Dilys, Beth and Unity were
all bawling, but Evan could not afford to do so.

The hymn was a call to arms, which glorified the
soldier, the passion of war, celebrating victory of
good over evil, bloated with the imagery of blood. The
whole of Evan's dilemma was stitched into the fabric
of that hymn and sung into existence by outstanding
harmonic voices. Machismo was like a caste in those
valleys: there was nothing a man could do to shake
it off. A wood spider was lowering itself down from
an awning on a silk thread and Evan poured all his
concentration into that, that feat of a tiny thing, strenu-
ously denying the effects of the choir malting the damp
air. He looked everywhere for distractions, settling
on Unity's bald, sinewy forearms folded across her
chest. But the choir was relentless in their demand
for his surrender, pursuing him to the precipice of a
fabricated past.

Then the song seemed to break up in mid-air, like

dry dead wood. The casket was loaded into the hearse and the melodic line taken up by the shuffling feet in the road. As Evan was thinking he had made it through the ordeal, another one presented itself. A royal military police Cavalier was parked behind a line of cars. The car sat like an alligator with its rear wheels in a ditch, snout raised, the radiator a mouthful of teeth. One thing he had to say about these people: they were a tenacious outfit – and surprised himself that he was not bolting for the back door.

Beth and Dilys made a move down the steps towards the Daimler. 'You go on ahead,' Evan said.

'Travel with us, Uncle Evan, in the main car.'

'I'm going to skip the service, if you don't mind.'

'Why?' Unity tightened her hold on his arm.

'It's a long story.'

'Tell me.'

'Not now . . .'

'I'm not going to see you again, am I?' she said, feeling Evan pull away from her grip. 'I've just found you and you're going to leave us again.' There was an edge of hysteria on the rim of her voice. Evan feared she might cry, astonished that anyone could be so upset over a prodigal uncle. It pleased him too. It pleased him a great deal.

'I will be out of circulation for a while. Would you do me a favour until I get back? Find my son and let him know he's got all these beautiful cousins. Would you do that for me, Unity?'

The cortège began to move. Unity managed an affirmative nod of the head before she was swept up by the undertow of mourners.

Evan loosened the knot of his tie and descended the steps to the street. He dodged the crowds jostling for grid position and walked over to the provost's car. He reached out for the door handle and looked up at the red brick crematorium on the hill, its white doors opening on automatic hinges like a supermarket, in anticipation of a big flock of mourners. An earlier funeral party were being discreetly discharged out of a side exit. In this game, where one man's hot ashes kindled another's cold flesh, you could not tell for sure that you had your father and your father only in the urn they gave you at the end of the day. Yet Evan quite liked that idea, of a generic pile of ash: Reynold and his generation all in one jar.

He opened the door and slid into the rear seat. The two RMPs in front swivelled around quickly, their eyes bulging with strident confusion. 'Good morning,' said Evan.

'Jesus!' The provost sergeant tossed a cigarette out of the passenger window and swallowed hard. 'You've been giving us the run around, Captain . . .'

'They're burying my father today. I didn't want to go to the service. I want to go to Aldershot instead.

That's what he'd want me to do anyway.' He felt an indifference to the military rituals of dishonour he was about to go through, for he no longer believed in their system of honour. He would be like a voyeur sitting in his own court martial. But he did feel a court martial to be necessary. Two deaths in Northern Ireland needed a valediction. Three deaths, counting the infant. 'So Aldershot it is then, gents, and don't spare the horses.'

The sergeant came and sat in the back with Evan. He had tattoos on his forearms: MOTHER inscribed on the left, FUCKER on the right. 'Another world up here, Captain,' he said, nodding at the hundreds of miners filing past the window.

'Years ago I didn't want to be in another world. I wanted to be where everyone else was. Now I'm not so sure any more. People here live out of time. Sergeant, was it you who punched me in the kidneys?'

'I'm sorry, Captain, but you were resisting arrest.'

'That's all right, Sergeant.'

His father's cortège ascended the hill behind them, an elegant carnival half a mile long. He heard the distant voices of the choir in motion grow shrill and imagined he heard the crematorium sucking in oxygen. There was nothing morbid about it, he had had a good day. And the old man would always be there in the corner of his eye. Like a lighthouse over rocks, Reynold was something you needed to keep in sight, just to avoid. In any case, the big influence in his life was now coming from the son, not the father. It was hard to believe Terence had been conceived in such a casual, accidental way.

They left the valley as he had done ten years earlier, leaving one home to make himself another in the army. They had never managed to capture him. That he had given the military the slip for so long was a measure of how good a soldier he was. He could have gone on hiding in the wilderness with Terence indefinitely.

When Evan had been away in the military he had heard that women were in office, and fathers were bouncing children on their knees. None of this had touched him. It was the one revolution the army didn't engage in. Society evolves, but its army remains a static metaphor for manhood in its most rigid and malevolent form. Soldiers are dinosaurs.

At the beginning of the decade, Evan spent a Christmas Eve with four senior NCOs from Two Para locked in an empty park in Hammersmith, London. Together they drank huge quantities of Bourbon and rum. He just couldn't get enough. This was paradise. Evan had just got his wings three weeks previously and there he was, drinking with four old dogs of war, glamorous men he wanted to emulate so badly. The significance escaped him at the time, but all they really talked about was their estranged wives, children. 'I played soccer with him right under this tree,' was one lament in the dark. 'That was in 1977. I haven't seen him since.'

Now he knew what the price was, of membership in a knuckle-headed battalion. The price was to forfeit the right to a natural life on the civilian side of the wire. The Parachute Regiment became family subsequently; his father was correct on that point. It was a family of men without women or children, who trusted one another with their lives. The genesis of this affection was violence however, and only through violence could that affection be sustained.

The provost car began to feel like his hearse bearing him back to a living death in Aldershot. He felt his earlier confidence eroding fast. Fear was beginning to take its place. The RMP driving the car, a corporal, pulled into the last petrol station in the valley. It was owned by Parry Jenkins, still trading even though his custom had become an occasional luxury. He still offered a personal service, pumping the petrol himself, checking the oil. As he wiped their windscreen, Evan saw how Parry Jenkins had grown old. He had to be in his seventies now. His jaws drooped like a basset hound and he couldn't move around the forecourt as fast as he was once able. He wore a bright red scarf around his neck and navy overalls. Exactly what he always wore, in fact, ten . . . twenty years ago. Then Evan remembered Parry Jenkins used to keep birds of prey. He was suddenly excited to know if he still had them. He asked to leave the car on the pretext of stretching his legs before the long haul to Aldershot.

The sergeant came out of the car, straightening his khaki shirt sleeves, which were rolled up so perfectly they looked made that way. He followed Evan who strolled up to old man Jenkins. 'Do you still keep the hawks, Mr Jenkins?' Evan asked.

Parry Jenkins squinted and looked at Evan as though he should know him. 'Aye, I do as a matter of fact. I've got a creature round the back to beat all creatures.'

Evan and his escort walked behind the garage to where there was a shed with a green door. He peered through the window, but all he could see in there was a leather thong hanging down from a chrome clothes rail and some feathers on the floor. As he stepped back the sergeant gave out a little yelp. Evan spun round and saw it. Chained to a log five feet away was an eagle owl, four feet tall with ears like a cat and bright orange eyes. In its talons was a tawny owl, midway between life and death. They had interrupted its dinner. The eagle owl stopped tearing the flesh from the bone and frigidly compressed its plumage. Evan filled his lungs with its atmosphere. He felt like a boy just staring at it. The bird seemed to sweat the youth out of him. It was a preposterous, amoral creature, feeding on its own kind. Evan just couldn't take his eyes off it and thought nostalgically of Terence. He would have loved the boy to see this. It was so full of life, like a great work of art.